"You're no...

He turned, just ... glower. "And quit looking at me that way."

"What way?"

"You think I won't bite your head off—I will."

"Go for it," she urged him. "Bite."

Suddenly he grabbed her. His hands were rough on her shoulders. He yanked her closer. His mouth slapped on hers, communicating pressure and dominance. He was one pissed-off kahuna, all right.

Still, she didn't back off and she didn't kick back. She did what any other lunatic of a woman would do.

She melted. Right into him. Feeling the rush of sensation when his kiss darkened, deepened, took.

When he suddenly jerked his head up, she just might have fallen if he hadn't still been holding her.

"My God, you're trouble," he grumped.

"Watch it. Compliments go straight to my head."

★★★

Become a fan of Silhouette Romantic Suspense books on Facebook and check us out at www.eHarlequin.com!

Dear Reader,

In real life my kids were lucky to survive my cooking. One time, just trying to boil water, I nearly burned the house down. Another time I tried a new recipe that even the dogs wouldn't eat.

But in fiction I get to play...and this story gave me a chance to play with fabulous, interesting food. My heroine's knowledge of food enables her to identify a murder—even if no one else could see it. And my hero, of course, never knows what hit him from the time he first meets her.

This story was so much fun to write—murder, mayhem, Alaska, gourmet delicacies and a hero and heroine who are so, so positive they couldn't possibly belong together.

I hope you enjoy.

Jennifer Greene

JENNIFER GREENE

Mesmerizing Stranger

ROMANTIC
SUSPENSE

If you purchased this book without a cover you should be aware that this book is stolen property. It was reported as "unsold and destroyed" to the publisher, and neither the author nor the publisher has received any payment for this "stripped book."

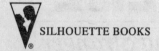 SILHOUETTE BOOKS

ISBN-13: 978-0-373-27696-7

Recycling programs
for this product may
not exist in your area.

MESMERIZING STRANGER

Copyright © 2010 by Alison Hart

All rights reserved. Except for use in any review, the reproduction or utilization of this work in whole or in part in any form by any electronic, mechanical or other means, now known or hereafter invented, including xerography, photocopying and recording, or in any information storage or retrieval system, is forbidden without the written permission of the editorial office, Silhouette Books, 233 Broadway, New York, NY 10279 U.S.A.

This is a work of fiction. Names, characters, places and incidents are either the product of the author's imagination or are used fictitiously, and any resemblance to actual persons, living or dead, business establishments, events or locales is entirely coincidental.

This edition published by arrangement with Harlequin Books S.A.

For questions and comments about the quality of this book please contact us at Customer_eCare@Harlequin.ca.

® and TM are trademarks of Harlequin Books S.A., used under license. Trademarks indicated with ® are registered in the United States Patent and Trademark Office, the Canadian Trade Marks Office and in other countries.

Visit Silhouette Books at www.eHarlequin.com

Printed in U.S.A.

Books by Jennifer Greene

JENNIFER GREENE

lives near Lake Michigan with her husband and an assorted menagerie of pets. Michigan State University has honored her as an outstanding woman graduate for her work with women on campus.

Jennifer has written more than seventy love stories, for which she has won numerous awards, including four RITA® Awards from the Romance Writers of America and both their Hall of Fame and Lifetime Achievement Awards.

You're welcome to contact Jennifer through her Web site at www.jennifergreene.com.

To Lil
I wish you all were so lucky as to have someone
this uniquely special
in your life.
Love you, Lil. In the next life, hope I can be
more like you.

Chapter 1

In the army, Harm Connolly had developed a reputation for trouble. Not for getting into it, but getting out of it, and he was most attracted to trouble when the odds were against him.

Temporarily, though, impossible problems didn't strike him as any fun at all.

For the first time in his life, he couldn't find his guts. He really, *really* wanted to disappear in a deep, dark cave under an assumed name where no one could possibly find him.

It was the boat.

Since he'd arrived in Juneau yesterday, the rain had gushed down in thick, drenching sheets, and still showed no sign of letting up. The rain didn't bother him. That he was cold and soaked didn't bother him, either.

But standing on the dock, staring at the 103-foot

yacht—ironically named Bliss—Harm reflected gloomily that he'd rather suffer a burst appendix, get married again, face a firing squad—*anything* but climb aboard.

He'd never liked boats. Didn't matter if it was a dingy or a luxury yacht. The idea of being trapped on one for the next two weeks was enough to give him shudders… and the funny part of it all was that the boat trip had been his idea.

The gray, relentless rain blurred any chance of clear visibility, but Harm still kept his gaze homed on the four men climbing aboard ahead of him. They were all brilliant—a ton smarter than him—yet they'd become his employees a mind-boggling few weeks ago.

They'd sucked up to him from the get-go, but with each other… Hell. This morning, typically, none were speaking to each other. Enough friction sizzled among the four to fry a hole in the ozone. The silent anger pouring off the men was so toxic that it was bound to combust unless Harm somehow found a way to identify and defuse the source. Soon. Damn soon.

The yacht staff—captain and mate—greeted each of the men and ported their gear. Harm was last by choice. He wanted to board that boat like he wanted to cuddle up with a hornet's nest. Still, if he had to find something positive about this incredible mess…at least there were no women around.

When push came to shove, Harm didn't doubt his ability to handle financial crises or catastrophes or unexpected avalanches.

He was pretty good at handling most anything but estrogen.

"Mr. Connolly—Harm! Welcome aboard!" The captain, in full rain gear, surged forward and extended his hand. "Hope your trip into Juneau was pleasant. Nice weather for whales, huh?"

Harm was beginning to recognize Alaskans' unique brand of humor, and even wet and raw, the captain's smile was deferential. Harm got mighty tired of people treating him as if he walked on water, but in this case, he didn't mind the wary respect. Naturally, he'd thoroughly researched Ivan Gregory before signing on for this trip.

The captain was thirty-eight, of Lithuanian descent, a man's man with a history of hard drinking, womanizing and maverick morals—but Harm didn't mind a man's faults as long as he knew what they were. The critical factor was Ivan's experience. The captain knew the seas around Admiralty Island like the back of his hand, and had an unbeatable track record for sailing his way through rough weather, always bringing home passengers and boat undamaged.

"It was good to meet your men." Ivan grabbed his duffel before Harm could reach for it. "Interesting group. My crew is especially looking forward to this trip… we'll get your gear taken below, give you some time to wander about and get familiar with the ship…"

"That sounds fine. Thanks." Harm tuned out the captain's small talk as he stepped aboard.

He'd seen pictures, done his homework, of course, but was still startled by the reality of the boat's interior.

Peeling off his wet hood and jacket, he noted the aft deck was big enough to hold a board meeting. Double doors led into a spacious salon, the inside wall paneled in wild cherry, the cabinetry done in a rich burl. The leather seating clustered midroom was framed by bookshelves, all stuffed with books and references on Alaskan lore. Harm was just leaning closer to study the signed oil painting on the inside wall when his head suddenly shot up.

For an instant, he thought he heard a soprano. A woman's voice, emanating from the next room off the passageway—the entrance to the dining area.

But his attention was immediately distracted by the shock of hearing laughter from his team. His four guys were all peeling off their wet-weather gear, same as he was, but they were suddenly talking, clearly surprised and enthralled with the comforts of the yacht, sounding animated about the trip ahead. Harm wanted to hold his breath. He had no illusions the camaraderie would last, but it was a beginning—the whole reason he'd put this trip together. All four of them, he believed, were good men. Or had been good men, once upon a time. This trip was a chance to see if there was a prayer he could pull them back together.

Ivan pushed up his captain's cap and was clearly trying to channel the group's attention. "Okay, everyone, Hans here is my first mate." He motioned at a spectacled, gray-haired man who looked like a quiet grandfather type. "Cate's our chef this trip. You'll meet her shortly. Hans, in the meantime, will take you below, help stow your gear and then give you a tour of the ship. The only place off-limits is the crew's quarters. Otherwise, you're free to go anywhere, and explore all you want. I'll be topside for a few minutes, calling the harbormaster. We'll lunch in the dining room at twelve-thirty and do some Q & A, fill you in on the schedule, safety features and all that. A-OK?"

Cate? Harm's head whipped around again. There'd been no woman's name on the crew roster. He was positive.

And then he saw her.

Actually, what he precisely noticed was her shrugging off the captain's attempt to cup her fanny as she hiked past him into the main salon.

She dodged the captain's move, smooth as silk, but Harm's gaze still narrowed. Since she was female, she was inherently a problem. The captain's behavior hinted there could be an additional awkward problems between employer and employee. Yet, determining how much difficulty she was likely to add to the trip was confounding because her looks didn't remotely fit the picture.

Her hair was blond, paler than wheat, and she wore it razor short, spiked up every which way. Maybe she'd gotten around to brushing it last year. Her clothes revealed the flat figure of a kid—skinny jeans, mocs, a long-sleeved T-shirt with the slogan Forget Love! I'd Rather Fall In Chocolate! If she reached five-three, Harm would be surprised. With no makeup and a patch of freckles on her nose and a downright stubborn chin, she looked young. twenty-four, twenty-five? And far more like a scrapper than a siren.

Yet the first mate, the well-past-Viagra-age Hans, gazed at her as if she were the sex goddess of the century.

Harm's warring men—Purdue, Yale, Fiske and Arthur—spotted her and got the same moonstruck look.

The captain obviously thought she was the sexiest thing to ever sail this sea or any other.

Harm wanted to shake his head. Were they all crazy? She was no dazzler. More like an underfed scruffy mutt.

Only then she smiled and said, "Hey, guys. I'm Cate."

His heart went slam as pitifully as all the rest. It was that ssslllooooowwww smile. That throaty voice. That incomprehensible "something" that sent a guy's testosterone soaring and ransomed his common sense.

Him, too, Harm thought gloomily. His heart was thumping like a puppy dog's tail; his equipment already standing to attention. Hell.

He'd known this trip was going to be a nonstop stresser, but he figured her presence on the boat was going to turn the next weeks into a nightmare times ten.

Cate greeted the group with an exuberant smile. She didn't have to pretend. It was easy to be happy; she'd known from the start that this two-week gig was truly a dream job. There were only two teensy exceptions.

There were way, way, *way* too many men.

And the captain persisted in thinking that a bite of the cook was a job perk.

Still, she'd never been one to let a couple inconsequential details bog her down, and continued with her intro spiel. "Hey, guys! I'm Cate. Cate Campbell. Like the captain said, I'm your chef for the trip. I trained in New Orleans under one of the best chefs in the universe, which isn't to say that I'll ever be that good, only that my goal here is to knock your socks off with some terrific food—starting with lunch today at twelve-thirty. Just take whatever seat you want in the dining room. And over the next hour, I'll try and track each of you down separately, make sure I'm straight on any food allergies or preferences you have. Okay?"

Oh, yeah, that was okay. When the five guests climbed aboard, Cate had gotten a good studying look at all but the head honcho…but this was their first chance to get a look at her. The boss man still eluded her, was shedding rain gear in the companionway, his face in shadow—but his four minions had front-row seats. They looked up, and the smell of testosterone suddenly clouded the clean sea air. Sprawled like wet rats in the cushy leather chairs, they suddenly straightened their postures. Heads nodded like bobbers.

She'd seen the response from men before. Her sisters claimed disgustedly that she was sexy even when she was down with a nose cold—which was both silly and untrue. But men were men.

Cats were so much easier to get along with.

"All right…I'm back to cooking. Only one other thing I want to say up front. I'm the god in the galley. I'm not your wife, not your girlfriend—you don't have to watch your language or your manners around me, and you don't need to help with a thing. But nobody touches my knives, my tools or my spices. Can't imagine why you'd want to, anyway. If you need something from the galley, all you have to do is ask. We square?"

More head bobbing. A little laughter. A lot of smiles.

"Okay, I'll catch up with each of you in a bit."

En route back to the galley, naturally, Ivan tried to cop another feel. She shot him a look so icy it could have stopped global warming in its tracks, then just moved past him.

She heard his muttered chuckle. "Sheesh, Cate, it wouldn't kill you to loosen up. Don't forget, we're in Alaska. Rules are a lot more flexible here."

"I'm positive I told you in the job interview that I flunked 'plays well with others' in kindergarten."

"God, I love a feisty woman," he said.

She kept on going, didn't even waste a roll of the eyes. The captain wasn't a serious problem. As far as she could tell, Ivan was a terrific sailor, just a jerk around women. She could handle him with both hands tied behind her back, and even if the other men proved to be mangerines—boys with unmanageable balls the size of tangerines—Cate didn't anticipate any sweat working with them, either.

She would hardly be an adventure chef if she didn't love a little risk and danger now and then.

She zipped into the galley, instinctively whistling some old kick-ass rock and roll. What a kitchen. She'd made dinner for seven in the Himalayas in a snowstorm, sand-roasted snake for a gay couple in the Amazon, so maybe cooking under adverse conditions was her forte—but man, there was nothing wrong with a little luxury.

Naturally, she'd brought her own knives and spices—what chef didn't?—but the galley was a techno dream. Armed with a hot pad and spatula, she checked on lunch, savoring the work space at the same time. The Corian countertops were in a sharp navy blue; the walls ice-cream white. A Thermador cooktop and grill accompanied the Sub-Zero fridge and freezer. Extras included the trash compactor, double sink, convection microwave and two—count 'em, two—Thermador convection ovens, and that wasn't even counting the to-die-for pantry.

The whole package was enough to give a girl multiple orgasms—without all the hassle and messiness of a personal relationship. Besides which, the job was going to leave her with a chubby chunk of money. How could a girl not whistle?

It took less than ten minutes to put the finishing touches on the lunch menu. Obviously, the first meal needed to be killer good. Not fancy. Nothing that guys would be afraid of. It just had to be exactly right.

Once those chores were checked off, she grabbed her list with the passenger names and hustled below to the guest cabins. The big shot, she already knew, was Harm Connolly. The first names of his guys were Fiske, Yale, Purdue and Arthur. At the first cabin door, she rapped, and waited.

The man who answered the door was short, white-haired, plump and out of breath. Fiske. She took one look at the kindly eyes, judged him to be good to the bone and smiled. "A lot of running around this morning?" she asked sympathetically.

"Glad to finally be aboard and settled," he admitted.

"I'll bet. And I'm not going to bug you, just want to ask a couple of things to make sure I have the right info. Do you have any food allergies? Or any food issues, cholesterol, diabetes, anything you didn't put on the form that I need to know about?"

"No allergies. Nothing but the usual boring health issues, either. A little heart issue, have to take cholesterol meds, should lose a few pounds, that kind of nonsense. Had to give up doughnuts." He added in a mournful tone, "I love doughnuts."

"Me, too," she confessed. "Rather have coffee or tea?"

"Coffee."

"Listen, Fiske, if you need a treat, you come find me. You hear? Or if there's anything special you like, just say." She resisted hugging him, but right off the bat, she could tell he was going to be an angel.

When she knocked on the next door, she knew she'd found Purdue even before the guy introduced himself. It was the look. Tall, dark, good-looking, maybe thirty, know-everything, so smart he charmed himself. In another ten years she figured the sharp edges might start showing up, but right now, he'd tickle any single woman's radar. Hers not included, of course. He had the posture of someone who was always tense, always ready to duck and run—or charge. Maybe he had good reason to never relax, she thought, and knew perfectly well all those prejudgments weren't fair.

"Just checking things off my list," she said cheerfully. "Do you have any food allergies or dislikes you didn't already mention?"

"Anything you make, Cate, I guarantee I'll like."

There were compliments, and then there was flattery. She'd never had patience for the latter, and was pleased to see him bump his head on the narrow cabin door when he turned around. At the end of the narrow corridor was a bathroom—head, she reminded herself of the correct term—and then rapped on the cabin door after that.

Arthur looked just like his name. He was easily six feet, maybe fifty-five to sixty, with a handsome head of premature white hair and a long face with stress-dark eyes.

"Any special things I can make for you, Arthur? Food allergies? Types of food you really don't like?"

"Nothing special, but I tend to get up early. How soon is coffee available?"

"Any time you want. I'll have a pot of fresh in the salon by 6:00 a.m. If you want it earlier yet, no sweat, just say."

"No, that's fine." Arthur seemed to look through her, not at her. Cate fully understood that some people treated staff as invisible, but Arthur appeared more preoccupied than rude or snobbish. She made a mental note to watch out for him, make sure she found things to tempt him at mealtimes.

The last aft cabin was hers—the sleeping area was the size of a closet, with an adjoining hatbox-size head. Normally, she'd sleep in the crew quarters, but when Ivan lost his regular chef and interviewed her…well, Cate wasn't about to sleep in a bunk in the open crew quarters, not when there was a spare cabin with a locked door.

On the starboard side, again she knocked…and the last of Harm Connolly's guys yanked open the door. Yale. Had to be. Easy to guess how the two youngest men had picked up Ivy-League-type monikers, no matter where they'd actually gone to school. Yale was blond to Purdue's dark, thin rather than muscular, and had a trimmed beard where Purdue was clean-chinned. Still, they both looked like up-and-comers, duded up with expensive labels and styled haircuts, in the same early-thirties age bracket.

"Hey," he said, giving her the same up-and-down that Purdue had—although not as offensively. Somewhere in that practiced expression was some honest friendliness. "Quite a boat."

"Fantastic, isn't it?" She reeled off her short list of questions.

"I can eat anything." He cocked his head. "You can't be on 24/7."

"I'm not. Once dinner's put away, I'm on my own time."

"So…you do have some free hours."

She wasn't about to pretend she didn't understand where he was going. "Tons. Crew and staff eat together, tour together when we're offshore. We'll all have plenty of time to get to know each other. Once the dinner stuff's completely put away, though, I'm on my own time. Which means you guys can stay up deck, drink all night, watch whatever you want and do whatever you want, without crew in your face."

"That's good," he said, then opened his mouth to continue.

"I'm en route to your boss," she mentioned, which shut him up beautifully.

Of course, it shut her up, too. Ivan had made clear to the crew that sucking up to Harm Connolly was required. Unfortunately, Cate had always flunked the course in kowtowing. It would have helped if she'd gotten a look at him before, she thought glumly, but no, she hadn't thought ahead and made the effort. Truth to tell, failing to think ahead was a fault of hers. In fact, pretty much a fault on a daily basis. And she really didn't want to put her foot in her mouth right off the bat with the head honcho...which meant she was all too likely to.

She rapped. Waited. Thought aha, maybe she could get a reprieve and not to have to deal with him right then—but then the door unlatched and there he was.

The punch in her gut was completely unexpected. He was the owner of a big-to-do company, for Pete's sake. Mentally, she'd had pictured him as in his sixties, tyrannical, formal.

Instead she got a half-naked dude with sculpted shoulders, unshaven cheeks, and a head full of towhead blond hair, spiky and wet from a fresh shower.

At least he'd pulled on pants before answering the door, but the technogear revealed the long, lean muscles of an athlete, not a desk guy. His eyebrows and chest hair were as white-blond as his hair, his skin ruddy. The glower of impatience on his brow radiated arrogance, energy. He couldn't be older than mid-thirties. And the sharp, dark gaze inhaled her in a single testosterone-colored photo snap.

His expression telegraphed that he knew what he liked, and he liked the look of her.

The overall punch was…well, downright bamboozling. It was more than his being unexpectedly hot. She just rarely, rarely got that suck-in-the-gut response for a guy. She loved men; what woman didn't? And she'd slept with them now and then, of course. Liked a good-looking ass, naturally. But she always carefully steered miles around the rare guy who brought on that suck-in-the-gut feeling.

She liked adventure. Hell, she loved risk.

She just didn't like risky men.

"You're the chef," he said, in a voice that sounded like rough gravel.

"Yes. And I don't want to bother you. I just wanted to ask you a couple of short—"

"Come in. There are a few things we should cover."

She didn't want to go in any of the boys' cabins. But she tapped her pencil on her list and sucked it up.

The master cabin was an awesome comfort zone—queen-size bed, teal carpet thicker than a lawn, teak cabinets for gear, an angled private head. Steam was still pouring from that bathroom, a thick white towel abandoned on the bed, all of it smelling like wet, clean male—intimate, distracting. Somehow there wasn't room enough for the two of them, even in the most spacious cabin onboard.

She backed up against the door, thumbed on her ballpoint and started with the questions, but he immediately interrupted her.

"I'll be fine with any food you serve." He radiated impatience, more than annoyance. "I need some meeting time with my staff. The dining room would work best because of the table size. When's it free?"

"Whenever you want it to be." Ivan would be proud of her. It was a kowtower's answer, even if her chin was already chucked up to hold her own. The man was too damn tall. Not counting his other faults.

"This is the deal. I want my staff to have a vacation out of this. Want to see them interacting in relaxed situations, onshore, offshore, meals and all. But I need to secure some uninterrupted time with each of them— with the door closed, just me and each of the men, for a good hour each day."

"So you specifically need the dining room then. Morning or night?"

"Morning. After breakfast. Obviously, that schedule will need to be flexible, depending on the trip agenda for that day."

"No sweat. Dining room's yours from nine until ten—or later if you want it. I do need to start setting up for lunch by eleven-thirty, ballpark. If that won't work for you, just let me know."

"Fine. Now, problem two. The captain told me you'd be sleeping down here."

She wasn't sure where he was headed, but somehow

she was already bristling. "Yes. If the captain didn't mention it, his usual chef is a man, who came with his son, who worked as a cabin boy. Normally, everyone bunks in the crew quarters. But when the chef had emergency surgery, the job came open for me—"

"I don't need all these details."

"I was only trying to explain that the crew quarters were set up for men. I mean, it's an open space, everyone bunking together. I could have done that if I had to, but I'd rather have some privacy, and you didn't book all the cabins, so there was the small cabin aft, has its own head. If you're afraid I'll be noisy—"

"I'm not afraid you'll be noisy. I'm afraid you'll be an awkward distraction." He took another impatient breath, looked away, then back at her. "Arthur's married. The others aren't."

"I have to admit, I think Fiske is adorable," she offered, referring to the oldest of his staff, but he just sighed at her attempt at lightness. Clearly, he had no sense of humor.

"This is the story, Cate. I inherited my uncle's pharmaceutical company when he died a few months ago. At the time I was living across the country, outside Portland, Oregon, but I moved, put the life I had there on complete hold. There just was no one else to take on Future, Inc. It was more than a family commitment. The company was in the middle of doing…extraordinary things. None of that is your business or your problem. But my situation is that my science management team is in the middle of a major crisis. I'm using these two weeks of being trapped on this boat to ferret out personalities, problems, solutions. But I've got my hands full without adding further complications to this…soup."

"Aw, shoot. I was planning to seduce Yale one night, Purdue the next and run down the halls naked between cabins at all hours of the day and night." Eek. He wasn't smiling. And suddenly she felt awkward as a prickly thorn. He'd shared something of a problem and she'd buzzed him off. If he hadn't implied she'd be a sexual distraction for his employees, she'd have behaved better. Darn it, Cate knew she got ticked off easily. So now she had to try to fix it. "I didn't mean to make light of a touchy situation. And I appreciate your filling me in. When you're working with your guys, I'll do my best to keep us all out of your way."

"It's you I'm concerned with. Not the rest of the crew."

Well, hell. He got her back up all over again. "Trust me. There won't be a problem," she said stiffly.

"I'm not trying to offend you."

"You aren't." He was.

"I'm just trying to make sure you aren't caught in the crosshairs of an awkward situation—"

"Trust me. I won't be." If her spine got any stiffer, she could have drawn a straight line with it. Above deck, she heard the engines start up.

He sighed. "Cate…I apologize. I can see in your face that I've handled this badly. I haven't slept in two nights—"

"You haven't handled anything wrong, and even if you did, you're the boss. But I need to head up now. I'll see you at lunch."

She ducked through the door, scampered topside and kept on going. That man might be stupendously good-looking and hotter than any man she'd known in the last decade. But so far, everything he'd said had rubbed her mightily the wrong way.

Still… Her spirits lifted as she neared the galley again. From the summer when she was eight—and lost her parents and whole world to a fire—she'd never depended on anyone or anything to make her happy. She could survive anything, and had. She never let anyone so close that a loss could destroy her.

Her heart was open, she thought, just not to hurt. An example of that was how hugely she planned to enjoy this trip. She saw it as an outstanding challenge, the chance to savor a fresh set of experiences, an opportunity to see yet another wondrous place in the world. Whether Harm Connolly was an annoyance didn't matter worth beans. She could put him out of her mind faster than a finger snap.

She had with every other man who'd given her a problem.

Chapter 2

Cate wiped her hands on the linen towel. Panic was setting in. It was a comfortable, familiar panic, when a meal was just about to be served, but still, a definite panic. Lunch was a naturally easy menu to pull together, but it was still their first meal onboard, their first exposure to her as a chef. It had to be perfect. In fact, by her standards, it had to be way better than perfect.

"You ready to serve, Cate?" Ivan started to step in the galley.

"Out," she snarled, then had to sigh when he threw his hands in the air in a gesture of comical apology. She could be nice. Really. She just didn't have that people-pleasing gene—but God knew, she tried. Seconds later, she popped her head around the corner of the galley with a brilliant smile. "Just sit down, y'all. I'm bringing it out as we speak."

And she did, one dish at a time. The first plate just held homemade bread, still steaming, accompanied by a fat scoop of mint butter. She'd chosen the asiago potatoes, because guys always—*always*—liked potatoes, and it was her own recipe with the bliss potatoes and specks of fresh chives and basil with the asiago cheese melted inside. The killer course was a thinly sliced skirt steak—if the guys didn't go for that, she'd have to commit suicide. She made it with heavy cream and blue cheese and baby spinach, lemon juice—fresh, of course—and a bit of shallot. The only problem with the whole meal was having to do 99 percent of it at the last minute. At least the fresh salad had been easy; all she'd had to do was add some hazelnuts and mandarin oranges to perk it up.

She started to relax when she saw the Gobble Factor kick in. Each of the guys took a bite, looked at each other…then started wolfing it down. Men were such pigs.

She was so glad.

She heard two rounds of "Oh, my Gods" before she allowed herself to sink into the chair next to Harm. The seating wasn't a choice. Cate had to be closest to the galley, and Harm and Ivan did the obvious male-posturing thing and had already claimed the two end chairs.

The minute they finished, she was prepared to bounce up and bring in dessert. It was an easy serve. She'd made peppermint cookies, her personal creation, and for those who wanted a heavier fare, vanilla honey-bee ice cream. For now, all she had to do was make sure no one needed anything. Ivan had the stage, was filling the guests in on the safety of the boat and the general lay of the land—or sea, as it were. There weren't many rules. "We'll get the safety drills out of the way. Then the boat's yours. We do ask that you stay out of the pilothouse unless invited. Hans and I like company up there. We'll ask every one of you to join us, but there isn't space for more than two at a time...."

She listened. Sort of. She'd had a week onboard before the guests arrived, but she'd been running full tilt to get her food on and organized. She hadn't paid a lick of attention to the safety stuff, primarily because she didn't care. Harm, she noted, was studying his men more than he was eating, and felt a sudden frown coming on. Tarnation, maybe he didn't like her skirt steak?

Ivan was onto the general itinerary by then. "Today, we'll be at sea, so it's a good afternoon to just relax, start soaking it all in. Chairs on both the fore and aft decks, with blankets and binocs. We're starting on the west side of Admiralty Island, and the first offshore stop will be tomorrow night, Tennehee Springs. Anytime we see a run of good fish, we'll stop, put our lines in. Any time we see whales or sea lions or bear, anything we run across, we drop anchor. You're not in the city now. We built in time to kick back. If you don't see a dozen eagles by this afternoon, I'll be surprised."

Cate took a bite of each dish. Par for the course, she wasn't particularly hungry. Obviously, she taste-tested whatever she made, but she was fretting more how the others were responding.

Next to her, Fiske, as expected, pounced on anything

sweet. Arthur devoured the potatoes, but wouldn't have helped himself to more if Cate hadn't unobtrusively passed the bowl again. Yale and Purdue presented no surprises; they wolfed down anything in front of them. Hans—Ivan's uncle and first mate—refused to acknowledge that he had a hiatal hernia. She always had to watch out for him. If he didn't eat slowly, he could suddenly start choking.

Ivan loved everything—his not being fussy was one of the few things about the captain's character she appreciated—and at least he didn't start with the liquor until after dinner.

Harm… She tried not looking at him again, but it wasn't her fault that he was sitting right next to her. Their eyes kept meeting. A total accident, she was sure, not interesting or meaningful or anything…but damned, if he didn't have killer eyes. Blue as the sea. Hawk eyes, narrowed, perceptive. For no sane reason in the universe, heat shimmered up her pulse.

What *was* it about the darned man that kept disarming her? Tons of guys were good-looking. It didn't make them any less problematic than the homely ones. Sometimes the opposite was true.

Still…the more she didn't look at Harm, the more she happened to notice that the shadows under his eyes spoke of a very real exhaustion. And unlike his staff, who were generally decked out with the most expensive labels REI and Patagonia sold, Harm's shirt was untucked, his pants wrinkled—as if he hadn't had time to do more than throw clothes in a suitcase. And he rarely took his eyes off his men.

And he still wasn't eating.

If there was one thing Cate couldn't stand, it was a man who didn't appreciate fabulous cooking. At least if it was her fabulous cooking.

She didn't see any sign of the huge problems with Harm's men that he'd implied, but she did pick up a bunch of information. The guys looked ultrabright for apparently darned good reasons. Plump Fiske was the financial VP. Tall Arthur was the head of "projects." Yale and Purdue were lead scientists. Cate wasn't sure what all that meant, but she gathered their lab was located in a quiet, wooded area somewhere outside of Cambridge, and that they created some serious, heavy-duty medicines.

The tension around the table only turned itchy when the subject of some new cancer treatment came up. Cate sensed that easily enough, but more, she was stuck rethinking her first impression of Harm. Sure didn't sound as if he were just a money monger or a suit. He was obviously involved in something real and serious.

Once she got that, she started studying his staff the way he did. In two blinks, of course, it was obvious the men weren't behaving like bosom buddies. Yale and Purdue had to compete with every breath. One couldn't eat a bite without the other trying to eat two. Fiske tended to act like an abuse victim, not cowering exactly, but stellar at being invisible. He didn't contribute to the conversation unless dragged into it. Arthur spoke only of the trip, what they were going to see and do, nothing of business or outside life.

And they all sucked up to Harm. Would he like this,

would he like that? Had he done this, would he like to do that? They piled it on so thick, Cate didn't figure a shovel could get through it.

Eventually, though, they'd leveled lunch, including a complete annihilation of her peppermint cookies. By then, she'd already leaped up twice to serve coffee and tea, and finally sank back in the chair to enjoy a cup herself, when she abruptly realized the table had gotten quiet. She glanced up, suddenly aware the whole group was staring at her.

"What? What?"

"We're in love with you," Yale said.

"Completely. All of us," Purdue contributed, with serious passion in his voice. "We want to be with you. Forever. All of us."

She grinned. "Yeah, I know. That's what they all say. And if you think you liked lunch, wait until dinner."

Cate never left a galley—never left any kitchen—until the counters shone like mirrors, but after that she sneaked away for a break. Since the rain stopped, the men had been freely wandering around the boat, but after that she moved with the stealth of a thief. Once the rain stopped, the men had been wandering freely around the boat, but none of them had discovered the upper-upper deck over the pilothouse yet.

It was all hers.

Although no one would ever know it—it was forbidden—she'd been sleeping up here every night unless it rained. At night, it was colder than a well-digger's ankle, but she didn't care, didn't care that the narrow white deck was slick with rain right now. She leaned on the rail, just breathing in the breathtaking view. Damn, but this really was Alaska.

Mountains speared up from the endless sea. A watery sun painted the water with the sheen and depth of black diamonds. Tufts of emerald-green softened the craggy land masses, and pines reached tall enough to touch the sky. She spotted an eagle, then another, perched high and regal, reigning over their kingdoms. The air was so fresh it stung her lungs. Something leaped in the water... something bigger than she was. She snuggled deeper into her old Sherpa fleece and inhaled the peace.

Sometimes, rarely, she remembered the god-awful time when her parents died, the fire, the night she and her sisters lost everything they'd ever known or loved. Lily and Sophie dwelled on it more than she did. Cate still experienced the loss in nightmares...but moments like this reminded her what enabled her to build a life alone, no matter what it took.

The big yacht barely made a sound as it skimmed through the water. Everything around her was extra-ordinarily quiet, extraordinarily huge. A person seemed awfully small in a landscape this isolated, this totally wild. The smells, tastes, sights and sounds were all exotic, all breathtaking.

She was still savoring the scenery when she suddenly heard voices below. Loud voices. Angry voices.

She held her breath, listening, confused as to where the sounds were coming from—inside the boat, for sure, but not as close as the pilothouse or galley. Maybe from the dining room or salon just beyond that. She wasn't close enough to make out any specific words, but the nature of conversation filtered through. Two men were talking.

Incorrect thought, she decided. They were fighting.

And they weren't just a little angry with each other. From the tone, from the nature of voices, they were both furious. Rage-furious. Vicious-furious.

She gulped, then gulped again. She told herself that people argued all the time. Some people fought nice; others fought mean and loud. And men sometimes used anger like fiber, just a way to clear out their systems, an easy purge.

But the way her pulse rate was suddenly hiccup-ping—as if adrenaline was shooting up her veins—she knew this wasn't likely some impassioned argument about politics or ball scores. Something was wrong, really wrong.

A thump indicated that something was thrown. Then…more loud voices.

Then nothing.

A spank-sharp wind slapped her cheeks as she barreled down the ladder. In the next life, when she got around to growing up, she wasn't going to interfere in other people's business—ever. But right now she was afraid that thump meant someone had been hurt, and could need help.

That was stupid thinking, she knew. Even if the fight had turned physical, dangerous, she was the last person who had the power to stop it. The problem was, she might well be the only outside person who'd heard it. And the other problem was that she'd never had a brain when someone could be hurt. It was a genetic flaw. Back in school, she'd see a kid hounded by a bully and she'd hurled herself onto the bully's back, come home bruised and wincing.

She should have learned.

She slid open the door to the salon—and found nothing, except for a chunky book about Alaskan birds on the carpet. It was definitely a sacrilege, in her view, to throw such a gorgeous book, but there was no other sign of a struggle, no blood, nothing.

Shaking her head, she stalked through the dining room into the galley. The argument had made her uneasy, oddly shaken.

Cooking was the answer. Cooking was always the answer. The galley was her nest; she already knew every nook and cranny. Although it was still too early to start dinner prep, she could at least start messing around.

If she couldn't quiet her nerves, she could at least concentrate on food.

Her theory on the dinner menu was that the guys would need absorbers. It was the first night out, so men being men, they were likely to drink. She'd thumbed through her recipes, looking for food that was easy on the stomach, not too heavy, and settled on pasta puttanesca. The wine choice was still a question, but she'd about decided on a Montenegro.

Ivan had given her a separate budget for the dinner wines. He'd been stingy, but she knew her wines and how to stretch a dollar. The reds from Provence were predictably good….

The galley door suddenly slid open. She must have

jumped five feet, even though she could have sworn she'd completely calmed down.

"I know. You've got a rule about intruders in your galley. But I was hoping you might have a bandage."

Harm stood there with a hand over his neck where she could see blood between his fingers.

"What on earth did you do? Get in here!" Men. Such idiots. She pulled open a drawer, grabbed a clean white towel, then pushed his hand away when he failed to remove it fast enough. That close to him, her hormones gave an instantaneous buck, which she tried to ignore. "Who taught you to shave? Attila the Hun? These days we use razors instead of axes."

"I just figured I'd try to look more civilized before dinner. But it seems I packed an old razor because the blade sure seemed dead."

"You think?" There were no chairs in the galley, just a stool wedged under the counter—which she pulled out and motioned him to sit in. Impossible for her to get a good look at his neck if she was stuck balancing up on tiptoes.

"It's nothing," he said. "I just couldn't stop the bleeding."

She edged between his legs, took a good look at the cut, then reached above his head for the first-aid kit. "I know it's nothing. But you're still getting antiseptic, and yeah, a bandage. Did the blade have rust on it?"

"I don't think it was that old." And then, when he saw where she was reaching, he muttered, "Good grief."

She grinned. Her first-aid kit did rival a complete trauma unit. "Yeah, I know. But the thing is, I've got a collection of knives that would make a gangster proud. When a girl works with knives for a living, she unfortunately tends to get cut once in a while, so naturally I'm prepared."

Instead of sounding reassured, his voice took on a punch of panic. "Wait a minute. What are you going to do?"

She had to chuckle. Only then… She looked at him. She'd stepped between his legs to get a better view and angle on his cut. There was nothing odd about that. It was only now, she realized, that her outer thigh was grazing his inner thigh. And her palm cupped the side of his face, not unlike how a woman would cup her lover's face for a kiss. And his eyes were on hers, her eyes on his, with enough electricity to crackle up a fire or two.

Where the patooties had that come from?

"Hmm," she said, and stepped back fast.

The instant she let up pressure, unfortunately, the scrape on his neck immediately started bleeding again. It needed to be cleaned. Then she had to wait until the moisture dried before applying antiseptic. That had to dry before a bandage could conceivably stick, so that took another wait. Obviously, none of those minor actions took long…but all of them took touching him. She was close enough to smell and sense and see. To be aware.

Too aware. So she started asking him nosy questions. She sensed he wasn't normally into chatting up strangers, but maybe he was just uneasy enough around her to open up. Either that, or he was actually interested in spilling about his company and his current situation.

"So," she started out with, "is your first name 'Harm' symbolic of what you're like to be around or what?"

He chuckled. "Nothing that interesting. Harm is just a Dutch name. Means *ruler* or *leader* or something like that. My dad was Scottish, my mom Dutch. Inherited stubbornness from both sides, or that's what the parents claim."

"Are they right?"

"I plead the fifth."

It was her turn to smile. "So what's the deal with this company of yours?"

He took his time answering, but eventually, out it came. "I never anticipated having anything to do with the company. That's the problem. My uncle's name was Dougal, hit a mother-lode lottery when he was twenty-five. He was only married a couple of years when his wife got cancer, pancreatic, which is one of the wrong kinds, the kind where there's just not a lot of hope. Anyway, he was nuts about her, and that's how it all started—he was supposed to be an engineer, but when she died, he poured everything into a research lab, determined to find a cure. Didn't know shoes from shinnola when he first started."

"But he learned?"

"He more than learned. He spent his life at it, and like I said, Connollys seem to have that particularly stubborn gene. The first really great drug he patented over twelve years ago. By then he was almost broke, but that brought in a new flood of money. He wasn't interested in living high. He wanted the infusion for the research. The two areas he never stopped targeting were pancreatic and ovarian. Just when the lab had come up with an outright miracle drug, he fell ill. And right after that, the guys came through with an even more incredible breakthrough."

"For one of the biggies he cared especially about? Pancreatic or ovarian?" It was a relief when she could step away from those eyes, that skin, the feel of him. She piled the first-aid supplies back in the box and whirled around, happy to talk—but with a little distance between them. It wasn't as if she couldn't find dinner chores to work with by then.

"Pancreatic. Two new drugs had passed FDA by then, and a brand-new one—the best, a true miracle drug—was a pinch away from the last clinical trials. That's when Dougal died. I knew he wanted me to have the company, to continue with his work, but man." Harm scrubbed the back of his neck. "I was in the military. Mechanical engineer. Built bridges, roads, had a ton of math but never much straight science. Only my uncle, he had a terror of the firm getting sold, falling into the hands of certain pharmaceutical corporations—he wanted it kept in the family, with people who had the same goals, to conquer this cancer thing. Not to just be about profit."

"So he passed it on to you…." She put a little plate in front of him because that's what she did—fed people. A few wedges of bread, fresh herbs in a dip for him to dunk, one of the hors d'oeuvres she'd put on in the salon in a bit.

"Yes. Only the will was barely read—I'd just found a

place in Cambridge, wasn't unpacked—when the clinical trials for BROPE, the new drug, disappeared—"

"BROPE?"

"Bright Hope. The guys named it—"

"Okay. Got it. So the drug was stolen?"

"No. The trials were. The data. The proving data. *Damn,* this is good—" He motioned to his decimated plate. "Anyway, that crisis took place my first week. Then Fiske, our financial guru, comes into my office the next week looking gray and sick. The funds allocated for the last trial disappeared. They exist on paper. There's no record of anyone unauthorized—or authorized— touching the account. Only the money's gone. And Fiske is beside himself, worried I'll accuse him."

She rolled her eyes. Just like a child, he was holding out the empty plate, begging for more. "But you didn't?"

"No. There's no way Fiske did anything wrong. Fiske is good to the bone. Can't say he's a twenty-first-century economics man—he was my uncle's crony in age, old-fashioned in his thinking. But he'd have gone to the wall for Dougal. They were like brothers. But to sum up this cyclone—I've got this company that on paper is thriving beyond all anyone's expectations, with a cure for pancreatic cancer, a real damn cure, on the cusp. Reachable. Only now the whole thing is at risk. Someone inside has to be the problem, but it's not that easy figuring out the who. Yale and Purdue claim it was their research that was suddenly obliterated, so they'd hardly be guilty of any wrongdoing. They've been set back several years. And Arthur claims he'd been pushing Dougal for more careful recording and reporting practices for years, couldn't get anyone to listen to him, so finding him guilty doesn't make any sense, either."

"And there's no one else who could be the thief?"

"Not really. There's other staff, but they're clerical or broom pushers, some apprentices coming up. But no one who had access to those studies, the specific private lab or those computers. The thing is, over time, the whole formula could be recreated, but that'd be a matter of years. And literally millions of dollars. Probably more than millions."

"Eek," Cate murmured.

"Yeah. That's what I've been saying."

"So you're in quite a mess." She wasn't exactly alarmed when he lurched up from the stool. It was just that her heart rate tripled when he stepped toward her. His eyes were on hers, a flash of flirting, a flash of stark, sharp sexual intent. Thankfully, she saw his hand aim for the bowl on the counter before she leaned into the kiss she thought was coming.

She slapped his hand.

"A major mess," he agreed—although he tried one more time for a lick of batter from her bowl. Then he gave up, eased away, got serious again. "I closed the lab for a couple weeks. Took them all here. None of us can escape from each other, not on this boat, in this environment. I had to do something. This was the best choice I could think up."

She nodded. "I think you made a great move. That's

what I do with a soup sometimes. Put the ingredients together, then just let it cook, see what happens."

"Something will."

She nodded again. "Something has to happen. When you mix ingredients together, the tastes start blending. Different flavors show up. Flavors that never existed before."

"That's what I need," he said grimly. "Something to force...new information. To bring more out in the open."

"Harm..." She couldn't believe he had the nerve to go behind her back with his finger. This time she just motioned for him to remove his hand. He tried giving her a meek, apologetic look—but he couldn't sell "meek" in this lifetime. "I heard something this afternoon. The fight? You heard it?"

He quit playing around. "What fight?"

"Two men. I don't know which two, but they were really going at it." She rinsed her hands, wiped them on a linen towel. "At first I thought everyone would have heard them. But then I realized, of course no one would have, below deck—or in the pilothouse, with those doors closed and the engines going. Still. You didn't hear anything at all?"

He shook his head. "After lunch, I grabbed a catnap. Hadn't slept in two days. I went down so deep I wouldn't have heard a cannon." He cocked his head. "You didn't see who it was?"

"No. But, as you may have noticed, I'm not the shy, retiring type. A little argument wouldn't have bothered

me. I'd never have thought twice about it. But this fight...
it was...wrong."

She'd have said more, but the side door to the galley
suddenly opened. Ivan popped in, his jaw dropping when
he saw Harm in the galley with her. "Hey. You letting
the guests get hors d'oeuvres ahead of me? Where is the
justice in life?"

She shooed them both out, snapping her towel,
warning they'd get no food at all if they didn't let her
get back to it. By then, she had to buckle under and get
serious about her dinner prep. But her conversation with
Harm still troubled her.

It was over, she supposed. There was nothing else
she could have told Harm, beyond what she'd overheard.
It was his problem, and he already knew he had a big
problem. There was nothing she could help with or do
anything about.

But it worried her, once he'd let out how huge the
stakes were. A cure for one of the scariest cancers. That
was big medical stakes. Big hope. Big money.

Big risks.

As she unlocked her knife chest and chose her
favorite paring knives—what her chef cronies called the
Sheep's Foot and Bird's Beak—she thought that Harm
didn't seem the kind of guy who let information slip.
Whatever he'd shared with her, he'd wanted to. Possibly,
she considered, he was trying to warn her again about
avoiding getting close to his men.

She started pulling out pots, cutting boards, ingredients, but an alarming thought kept going through her
mind. This trip was enabling Harm to get closer to his

team. The closer he got, the more danger he could be in himself.

The fury and tempo of the argument she'd heard earlier kept replaying in her mind like a mosquito bite that wouldn't quit itching.

It wasn't her business, she reminded herself, any more than Harm could ever be her business. That unexpectedly sharp buzz of attraction to him needed to be cut off at the pass, pronto. Cate was no idiot. Harm came from a completely different universe than her life.

So for once she was going to be good, just do her job and enjoy the trip, not interfere or nose into anyone else's problems—and stay out of Harm's way.

It was such a good plan.

Chapter 3

"Marry me, Cate." Yale had a foot cocked up on the priceless wild cherry sideboard. "I have a condo just outside of Cambridge. You can have it. You can have my life savings. My grandmother's wedding ring. My six-year-old BMW. Everything I have."

"That's sweet." Cate looked around the dining table. "Anyone willing to up the ante?"

"Me! Me!" Purdue was still hunched over the dessert, clearly trying to protect it from anyone else claiming thirds. God knew they'd all had seconds. "He's only got a condo. I've got a house. A kitchen with a Sub-Zero freezer and stuff. I'm not sure what all the appliances are, but I was told they were top-of-the-line. And...I put the lid down. When I remember, anyway."

"But she'd have to sleep with you," Yale pointed out. "See, that has to be a deal breaker for her right there."

Arthur choked. "Don't you boys ever have a sense of limits?"

"It's totally all right, Arthur," Cate assured him, as she thumped him on the back. "I've trained puppies before."

That set the whole group laughing yet again. Harm leaned back, as stuffed as everyone else, confounded by the teasing and jovial atmosphere around the table. It seemed impossible that one of them was a thief, had sabotaged millions of dollars—and lives.

Cate was the one who'd initiated the easy dinner conversation, enabled it, played to each of the guys as if they were keys on her favorite piano. She wasn't a manipulator, he mused. It wasn't like that. She didn't remotely come across as having any agenda—beyond wanting them all to enjoy her cooking. But she had some people skills that put Harm in downright awe. She'd brought down the tension level in his guys by about 900 percent.

"Where are you from, Cate?" he asked, when he could finally get a word in.

"Actually...nowhere." Just as she had through the whole meal, she spotted Arthur's empty cup and poured him a cup of coffee, then pushed the wine toward Ivan. "I came from a family of five. Mom, Dad, three sisters. All of us closer than peas in a pod. But there was a fire—we lost my mom and dad. I was the middle sister, around eight when it happened."

"Hey. That's seriously awful." Yale dropped his flirtatious tone, at least for that second.

"Yeah, it was," Cate agreed, in that clear-bell voice

of hers. "We had no family who could take us in, so the court took over, split us up. We were fostered three different places. It was bad enough to lose both parents, but then we were ripped from each other, as well. At least we all had decent caregivers, and we wrote each other—but we had to be grown-up before we found a way to actually see each other again. Still, we e-mail each other a couple times a week."

"Do you at least live close by?" Harm asked.

"No. Nowhere near. But we've built up a pattern of going back home—our original home, in Georgia—at Christmastime. Although this year that might change because Sophie, the youngest, just tied the knot a few months ago. I suspect we'll use her home base now."

"But you must have a home yourself," Harm persisted. "Somewhere you hang your hat."

There. For all her flirting and obviously being very, very comfortable around men, their eyes locked. He'd felt the same spark of ignition before. Something flashed in her eyes—as if the testosterone in the room hadn't bothered her a single iota. Until she looked at him and he looked back.

"I pay rent in a place in New Orleans. That's where I learned to cook, where I stayed the longest as an adult. So that's where I set up an address, a place to get the bills, store stuff. But basically, I'm as footloose as you can get. Have job, will travel. And love it."

Arthur and Fiske both focused attention on her now, although Fiske was the one who spoke up. "You don't want a home? You're a beautiful girl. You're not thinking about a husband, babies?"

"Sure. But as you guys can tell, I generally get my share of offers."

"Picky," Ivan said, with a cock of his captain's hat.

"Very," Cate agreed, and then, smooth as silk, diverted the conversation away from her again. "Fiske, I can tell I'm going to have to make a fresh batch of peppermint cookies just for you tomorrow."

Harm's oldest in command was reaching for the cookie dish—again. "It's not my fault, Cate. I've never tasted anything like these before. Can't keep my hands off them."

"That's what I like to hear." With a grin, Cate stood up. "Just want to tell you all now—breakfast tomorrow will be Ebelskivers."

"What? What on earth is that?"

But she just chuckled. "My secret. Trust me, though, it'll be worth getting up for. In the meantime…I'm going to go clean up my galley and get out of your hair. You can all start drinking and swearing and being pains in the keisters to your heart's content. Glasses and beverages are here…." She motioned the side door of the fancy breakfront, which opened to reveal an ice chest. "Leave any dishes right here. I'll deal with them in the morning. If y'all plan to walk around naked belowdecks, just so you know, I've seen it all before."

"Does that mean you're going to walk around naked, too, Cate?" Yale called after her.

"Are you kidding? I don't like to scare men or wild animals. You can count on me to be covered."

And she was gone, just like that—giving them all a view of her baggy pants and wild hair. Damn woman was as agile as a wood sprite, Harm thought. Full of herself, full of zest.

And every single guy tracked her as intensely as he did. Ivan watched her like a bird of prey. He'd gotten quieter with every drink. And his second in command, the grandfatherly Hans, was the next one to turn in and call it a night.

Harm wanted to. He stayed, though, waiting to see how his team related after Cate left. No surprise, their smiles faded out. Ivan stood up, groaned, wished everyone a good-night. Still, none of Harm's men budged. Eventually, a deck of cards emerged on the table. Someone—Purdue?—started up a game of hearts.

Usually, a card game was good for a lot of groans and moans and competition, but Harm could see what was going on. No one wanted to be the one to leave. No one wanted to either look guilty or miss what anyone else said. Suspicion and worry were eating them all up from the inside out.

For fifteen minutes, Harm listened to the silent snap of cards, the increasing grim silence in the room, and finally spoke up. "You all look like zombies, and I'm just as tired. So I'm guessing you're all still sitting here because someone has something they want to say."

It was tall, white-haired Arthur who spoke up, the one who never made waves, never invited confrontation if there was a prayer of avoiding it. "We all know there's a thief, Harm. We all know it has to be one of us."

Purdue pushed back his chair. "And we all want to know what you're going to do about it. It's driving us crazy. Not knowing where we stand with our jobs, with the company, with our reputations. With not knowing what's going to happen."

Yale, who could be counted on arguing with Purdue on whether the sky was blue, actually nodded. "We can't keep on this way. None of us can leave. We've all got too much at stake. But nobody can think with this cloud over our heads, much less imagine working together again."

Harm waited for Fiske to take a turn, but his financial officer waved off the chance. So Harm took the floor.

"What we're going to do—what I'm going to do—is figure out where the money is. Figure out who did it. And then put the lab together. My uncle built an outstanding team—but I believe we can make it even better. You're each uniquely brilliant. One of you got sidetracked. Not all. Just one."

Purdue said, "Okay, so that's what you want to do. But how are you going to do it? All of us feel it. That we're under a cloud of suspicion."

"Because you are—but I didn't put that cloud there," Harm said. "The thief did. And I'll tell you this. In the next ten days I'll know who it is."

They believed him. God knew why, but Harm saw the trust and reassurance in their faces. It seemed the right time to close down shop, and the group followed him below deck, all of them yawning and expressing exhaustion.

Harm was well aware that one in the group was a fantastic liar and unpredictably dangerous. But his main worry—his real crisis of a worry—was that the group was counting on him. The whole company—not even counting their cure for pancreatic cancer—would go down if he couldn't.

And once Harm got that in his head, he couldn't sleep. He tried to. Heaven knew he was beyond exhausted, and his cabin was as comfortable as a luxury hotel. The steady lap of water outside was soothing, hypnotic—or it would be for anyone without so many problems preying on his mind.

A couple of hours later, cranky and disgusted, he yanked on sweats and made his way topside. He just… wandered. He'd forgotten—or hadn't known—that it was never going to be midnight-dark in the summer here. The sky wasn't daylight-bright, more the dusky, pearl hues of a late twilight. The salon and dining areas were gloomy with shadows, only the gleam of occasional brass relieving the dimness. Outside, the air was crisp, the pilothouse as deserted and silent as the rest of the deck.

Harm kept ambling, seeking to find the highest spot on the boat so he could see the Alaskan night from the highest vantage point. Beside the pilothouse was another set of steps, leading to a small top deck. He climbed up, exploring, not looking for anything beyond a quiet spot with a view. He found the view…but he also found a five-foot-long lump of blankets already up there.

Initially, he assumed the dark bundle of blankets was just a cover for some kind of storage—until he stepped closer and saw a white oval in the middle of all those covers. A face. A pixie face with a gleam of annoyed blue eyes staring back at him.

"Do me a favor and don't tell on me."

A minute ago, Harm would have sworn nothing could have aroused his sense of humor. "Hmm. I sense blackmail potential. What exactly am I not supposed to tell on you?"

"I'm not supposed to sleep up here. No one is. And the last thing I want the captain to notice is that I'm not where I'm supposed to be at night."

Since this was getting more interesting—and for damn sure, more distracting than a fistful of problems—Harm hunkered down on his haunches. "I suspect Ivan would be happier than a kid in a candy store to discover you were up here alone."

"Yeah, there's that issue, too." She sighed. "This is the thing. I'm pretty seriously claustrophobic. Have been ever since going through that fire when I was a kid. None of my sisters can stand feeling trapped or locked in either, but I seem to have it the worst." She paused. "On the other hand, I'm not the only one wandering around in the middle of the night. So what's your excuse?"

"My excuse is that I seem to have given up sleeping. To add insult to injury, the less sleep I have, the stupider I get. So that's pissed me off even more."

"Ah, I'll run for the hills then. I wouldn't want to risk pissing off a hotsy-totsy corporate magnate."

"I'm not a corporate magnate."

"Well, you're certainly crabby, whatever label you want to call yourself."

His gaze narrowed with interest. "So why aren't you running away?"

"You think I should?"

"Everybody else does." It was her own doing that he ended up beside her. He could have stayed in that hunched position indefinitely. She was the one who lifted the blankets and unrolled a few extra feet of tarp. The tarp had obviously protected her from the damp deck, which she was willing to extend to him, as well.

Her kindness was definitely appreciated, because damn, it was cold up there. Only being half-prone next to her immediately provoked the idea of kissing her.

That idea had been growing on him since, oh, around a second after laying eyes on her. It'd be funny if it weren't so incomprehensible. Inheriting the business had sliced his sex drive in half—or that's what he'd been trying to tell himself. Since his uncle had died, he'd been hurling himself around the country nonstop, thrown into legal and ethical situations that just kept getting deeper and darker, so obviously, there'd been no time to meet a woman or form a relationship. Harm had rationalized for some time that all the stress had obliterated his sexual needs.

Looking at Cate forced him to recognize that need was alive and clamoring-noisy. And the more he felt the nearness of her, the more he realized that need hadn't been satisfied in a long, long time.

"You don't take nonsense from anyone, do you?" he asked curiously.

"Sure I do. Everybody does."

But he didn't. And he'd long wearied of people who took it from him. From school to the military, to the business crisis he was in now, people had always deferred to him. Always expected him to find answers, to come through. To not show weakness. Cate had challenged him from the start. It was refreshing…but yeah, a little unnerving. And rather than think about that unwanted sexual tug, he started a conversation. "What was your impression? Of my guys, the team at dinner?"

She leaned up on one elbow. "When you told me what the situation was, I specifically set the table with good crystal, the white tablecloth. Probably sounds silly to you…but I've always found that atmosphere affects behavior. I also think having strangers around your group—like me and Ivan and Hans—probably brought out more manners in your guys. People always behave better around strangers. Likewise, if you give boys mud and water, they'll end up getting dirty. Put on the crystal, and they'll tend to be more polite, to get along."

He said, "I don't know about the crystal. But you sure did something because you got them talking."

"Not real talking. Just polite talking. I was hoping the atmosphere would help you figure out the crux of the problem."

"Who my thief is."

She frowned. "Where the poison in your company is," she corrected him.

"Same thing."

"I don't think so. The person who stole the formula not only stole the formula. He betrayed the team, hurt the other players—financially and job-wise—and is doing a pretty effective job of tearing down the company. Your uncle had lofty goals. So did they. The one who ripped that open took away some serious big dreams and goals, as well."

"You've been thinking about this," he said slowly.

"Not really. I don't know anything. It's just...an interesting problem. If the person did this right after your uncle died, then your uncle's death must have provided them with an opportunity. Access. But I don't get at all *why* someone would have done this. I'd think your whole team would have made a lot of money if that drug came through. So there'd have been no reason to steal. And then you described this group working as a team for quite some time. Working together, hoping together. So he was willing to tear apart the team, his friends, for some reason that I sure can't imagine. I think you've got a guy on your hands who's really, really angry. Angry about something that means a lot more than money to him."

He absorbed what she'd said. He'd had no one to share the puzzle pieces with before—except for the P.I. company he'd hired, but they didn't know enough about science to evaluate the possibilities for the how and why of a formula theft. Harm already knew he'd likely have to figure this out himself.

Cate, though, had different perceptions than he did. And he found himself staring into those soft, liquid eyes. He was taken with her spirit, with her zest, with her fearlessness. But he was also concerned about letting her any closer—to him, to his men, to his problems. He didn't want her exposed to danger.

He wasn't positive she'd recognize danger if it bit her on the tush, which was possibly what prompted his change of subject. "Ivan give you any serious trouble?"

Instead of an answer, she smiled. "I'm not the kind of woman who needs protecting, Harm."

And then—proving irrevocably that she needed serious protecting—she reached over and kissed him.

Nothing much shocked Harm, not anymore, but this sudden streak of lightning startled him completely. A dank, chill night turned sultry out of nowhere. Her lips were soft and warm and sassy. Her skinny body gave off more eclectic tension, more edgy hormones, than an invitation from any woman he could remember. Ever.

She lifted her mouth moments later, opened her eyes, looked straight at him. If she was shaken, it didn't show.

"What was that for?" he asked, as if she hadn't just rocked his sanity.

"You're not really interested in me. I'm not really interested in you. But it's been there, that little…sizzle. So I figured it'd be a good idea if we got it out of the way so we could both quit wondering about it."

He almost denied that "wondering," but there seemed no point in lying.

"So you think that settled the issue?"

"That was the idea. To settle it. I didn't want it to be a problem for you. Or me."

Clearly, she didn't know him well enough to realize that he was morally, ethically and emotionally incapable of turning down a dare.

She was damned right. He wasn't interested in her. Didn't think for a second that she was interested in him. She was just…full of herself. And since she wanted to get something straight, he figured he'd better get something straight, too. Kittens shouldn't risk playing with cougars.

So that's why he kissed her. More or less because she'd kissed him, because...

Aw, hell. He forgot the reason the moment his lips sank against hers, and she sank back, back into that nest of warm blankets. Apparently, she liked playing with dynamite, because those light, lithe arms skidded up his shoulders, scooped around his neck.

He looked for caution. Brains. Fear. Nobody home there... All he found was naked curiosity and tantalizing interest and her returning his kisses as if she was determined to pile more tinder on an already thriving fire.

Her lips felt softer than a cushion. The taste of her was exotic and different and alluring. She made a sound, as if she'd found a new flavor of chocolate she liked. Opened her lips, invited his tongue.

Damn woman.

She arched her flat chest against him, pushed up a knee in a gut response to that kick of lethal hormones. It wasn't need bubbling up, Harm told himself. He didn't acknowledge need, didn't have time for need. That was something a man overcame to achieve what he wanted in life. So it couldn't be need.

He was just...curious. That was all.

Unwillingly, his eyes closed. It was her fault, her witchery, because her arms seemed to wrap him up in a place that wasn't cold or damp or needled with problems. For two seconds, he forgot about huge stakes and betrayal and embezzlement. He forgot about the women he'd failed in the past, the ones who'd failed him right back.

He forgot his own name.

She sipped and sucked. He tasted and teased right back. He rolled her on top of him, creating a tangle of blankets that he found some way to push aside. He had to get a grip on her. He had to run his hands down that lithe, skinny body, to see where on earth all that evocative, provocative power was coming from.

Only then...he found out. When he stroked down her spine, she parted her legs, rubbed against him. He turned into rock. He hadn't had a chance to turn into solid rock in a very long time.

He skimmed his hands back up, stroking the same bones and soft flesh, into that messy short hair. She made those soft, appreciative murmurs again, as if she'd like him for brunch. Dinner. Breakfast. An all-day meal.

And abruptly, he rolled her on her back again and shifted away from her. This was insanity. It just couldn't be happening. He never lost his head, not with a woman and not in life, ever.

And there she was, panting a little breathlessly—as he was, damn it. But her eyelids slowly opened, and there was a moment of stillness. Then her gaze narrowed and her body tensed. He didn't know what she saw in his expression, but it was obviously something that made her wary.

She said, "You get away with that once. Because that's probably what you do. Establish that you're the alpha wolf, no matter who you're with or what you're doing. But I don't do wolves, and I don't give a hoot about power. So don't you kiss me again unless…"

"Unless?"

"Unless you plain old want to. No agendas, nothing to gain, nothing to win, no power thing. Just wanting." In a real frump now, she coiled to her feet and gathered up a messy scoop of blankets. "Damn it, Harm. Now you've forced me into going below deck to sleep in that claustrophobic cabin."

"You don't have to go anywhere. I'll leave."

"No. This way, you owe me for being an arrogant clod. And just so you know—I'm a score keeper."

"Just so you know, I'll remember your orders."

She cocked her head, asked in confusion, "What orders?"

"That order about not kissing you the next time—until I want to."

She didn't respond, just whirled around and headed below deck. He'd gotten the last word in, he told himself, but long after she'd disappeared from sight, he was still sitting on the damp, cold deck, feeling both sexually frustrated and flummoxed.

What a piece of work she was.

But how fascinating.

Chapter 4

At 5:30 in the morning, Cate quit glaring at the ceiling of her cabin and gave up. She never had insomnia. Ever. But apparently, she was still too riled up about Harm to catch at any serious sleep, so she crawled out of the bunk and grabbed her laptop.

She didn't feel quite so claustrophobic by the port window. Outside, a shimmer of pale light dozed on the smooth waters as she turned on the laptop. She was way overdue e-mailing her two sisters. She was between the two in age, but her role had always been the caretaker. The tough one. They'd all been scarred and scared kids, but Cate saw the other two as more wounded. Someone had to watch out for them.

The note to Sophie, of course, had to be first, because her e-mail box was clogged with e-mails about how happy her sister was. It was enough to give Cate hives.

Enough was enough. Soph. You're not still on your honeymoon. For Pete's sake, you've been married almost six months. It's time for you two to have a fight. A real fight. How can I trust this guy if he doesn't behave like a normal male animal?

Then she pounded out an e-mail to Lily. I don't want to hear all the teaching crap. This is summer. I want to hear that you're out meeting guys, sleeping with guys, being irresponsible and impulsive. If you go to one more jewelry or Tupperware party, I swear to god I'm flying home to kick you in the behind.

There. Her sister-caretaking duties were done for the day. She closed her laptop, congratulating herself for getting her mind off Harm—and then noticed that only ten minutes had passed.

She tried a quick shower, thinking that maybe she could scrub the man out of her thoughts, but that didn't work, either.

She'd never been afraid of a man. No reason to be. She'd already faced the life stuff that was really terrifying—which was, cut and dried, losing everything that mattered to you. Guys didn't fall into that category. She could love them and walk away, just like she did possessions and places and everything else. Harm shouldn't be any different.

Only, damnation, he was. She wouldn't mind being attracted to a moneygrubbing hotshot, heavily into power and ownership and command and all that nonsense. That's what he was supposed to be. That's what she'd thought he was.

Impatiently, she towel-dried her hair, yanked on layers of merino wool and fleece, then slipped her feet into moc-boots. It was the way he'd kissed that threw her, she admitted to herself. She'd expected arrogance and selfishness. She'd expected him to be a taker.

Instead, he kissed as if he were a big old lonesome lion, who craved his own lioness to come home to, a cave of his own, the one place in a predator world where he could let down his hair.

As Cate climbed to the main deck, she almost let out a totally unfeminine snort. Harm in the role of romantic lion? Right. Annoyed the man was still entrenched in her thoughts, she was determined to concentrate on something else.

Like food. Food was always positive.

Ambling through the salon, the only sound she heard was the steady slop-slurping of water cradling the boat. As she passed through into the dining area, she found exactly the mess she'd expected—glasses and plates everywhere. She and Ivan had had a brouhaha before he hired her on. She was a chef, not a maid. Without a cabin boy, somebody was going to have to pick up the housekeeping duties. Eventually, they agreed—once he put more money in the kitty for her—that she'd clean up the dining room and galley 24/7. The rest of the boat was his problem.

She lifted the lid on the giant silver coffeepot—a treasure, old silver—and figured she'd grind Hawaiian beans today, add a touch of hazelnut...then scooped up a tray of glasses to cart into the galley.

She barely turned the corner before shock hit.

There was a long, bulky shadow on the floor. A body. A man's body.

The tray careened on the counter in a noisy clatter of glasses and silverware. She fell to her knees, put her finger on the pulse of his neck, then felt another shiver of shock when she realized his eyes were open.

She knew CPR. She was damned good at CPR. Unfortunately, CPR was too darned late to do any good. She recognized Fiske even before she knelt down—who else had that classic Santa-Claus figure? But it seemed impossible that he was dead. She'd just *seen* him a few hours before. How could that dear, gentle, quiet man who loved her peppermint cookies have died just like that?

Confusion suddenly made her freeze. It was a darned real question. How could he have died just like that? Obviously, he must have been seeking something from the galley in the middle of the night. But what? And he was crumpled on the floor in the oddest position, his hands framed in a cupped position around his neck. Had he choked? But on what?

If he'd slipped and fallen in the tight space of the galley, he would undoubtedly have hit a hard surface— yet there was no sign of blood or physical injury. If he'd choked, there was no sign of food or whatever he could have choked on.

She gulped, then jumped to her feet and hit the lights. She wanted Harm. To tell him first, to be the one to deal with this. But that was just her heart's instinct. Rationally, she knew her first responsibility was to contact Ivan. On a ship, the captain was the god, the law, and any other role that was stuck with bottom-line responsibility. She reached for the pager on the wall by the sink, her hands shaking as she hit the button for Ivan's cabin.

"What?" Ivan's voice was curt and groggy. No surprise, she'd wakened him.

"It's me, Cate. I'm in the galley. Fiske is here. I don't know what happened. But somehow…he's dead. I just found him."

Ivan muttered a curse, a sound of shock. Then, "I'll be right there. Don't do anything else until I get up there. Or…wait. Wake Connolly, would you? It's his man. We should tell him before anyone else finds out. And I'll be there as fast as I can get dressed."

She hung up, took one last long look at Fiske, and then ran. Her mind felt like a shaken box of Scrabble pieces, unable to form coherent words, make coherent sense. She pelted through the silent boat, belowdecks, then rapped sharply on Harm's door. He was undoubtedly sleeping. She'd probably have to rap more than once. Yet she hadn't even lifted her hand for a second knock when the cabin door opened.

Cate didn't panic. She never panicked. She wasn't the shaky, panicky type, yet Harm took one look, said, "Easy there," in a voice more gentle than silk. He pulled her in, pulled her close. "Bad news," he said, not wasting time framing it as a question.

She nodded, because her chin seemed to be wobbling too much to get a clear word out. It was his fault she couldn't keep it together. At least he didn't sleep naked, but he was only wearing sweat bottoms tied low on his hips. Her cheek seemed to be pressed into the geography of blond hair on his chest, which covered a far more muscular torso than a desk man should have. It's not that sex was on her mind. It wasn't. Even remotely. It was just…

No one did that. Held her. Just pulled her in and held her. And because Harm was so clearly braced for trouble, to take care of trouble, she didn't have to be.

"It's Fiske, Harm."

"Sick?"

"Worse. I found him dead on the galley floor. I paged Ivan right away, woke him up—he's probably en route to the galley by now. He asked me to come get you."

"Of course." But he didn't immediately release her, as if waiting to make sure she was steady again. He pulled back, blue eyes examining her face, shrewdly assessing how she was. "It's frightening. Finding someone who died. Happened when I was in the military too damned often. I don't care how tough you are. It's hard."

She took a big gulp, found the steadiness that had eluded her. Maybe she'd just needed him to say that she wasn't a wuss. "It was awful," she admitted, and then quickly turned around to face the door.

The instant Harm let go of her, he reached for the drawstring tie at his waist, obviously intent on dressing fast—whether she was there or not. "Could you tell what happened? How he died?"

She hesitated. "I've got some solid first-aid background, but I don't have any doctor-type judgment or experience—"

"Cate. Could you tell how he died?"

From the quiet urgency in his voice, she realized what he was really asking—if Frisk had died a natural death or if he'd been murdered.

Shock numbed her throat. She understood that the problems in his company were grave, but not that Harm had been worried about something like foul play or violence being a possibility. Suddenly, everything she'd seen and heard took on extra dimension. Her voice seemed to come out full of gravel.

"I don't know, Harm. There was no blood, so it didn't look as if he fell and hit his head. I…" She just couldn't force the picture back in her mind. "I can't guess why he was in the galley. Whatever happened must have occurred after you and I went below deck, so the timing had to be in the really wee hours of the morning." Her voice started to crack. "But I just don't know what a heart attack or stroke looks like, so I—"

"Okay. Damn. Didn't mean to make you feel put on the spot. The facts'll come out, Cate. It'll all get figured out. And I'm headed up right now." But before charging ahead of her toward the companionway, he snuggled a hand on her shoulder. It wasn't a sexual touch—just a totally personal one. A gentle squeeze of support, an awareness of how upset she was, even if she didn't show it. A gesture to let her know he was there.

Cate headed back on deck, thinking what a way to tick a girl off. She wasn't used to anyone being there for her. She didn't want anyone there, hadn't depended on anyone since she could remember—and liked it that way.

She damn near fell in love with the man over that single stupid gesture.

Of course, she wasn't herself. Finding a dead body was a mighty upsetting way to start a day.

If she wanted to wallow, though, there was no possible opportunity. Topside, Harm and Ivan took over the galley, locked in discussion.

Harm's men seemed to smell the crisis, woke up early, popped on deck one after the other, each appearing shaken by the news of Fiske's death. No one seemed to know what to do, what to say—and heaven knew, neither did she. But she just started pitching in, starting with making coffee, one pot, then another.

Even after Ivan and Harm headed for the pilothouse, no one wanted to be in the galley—not until some decision was made regarding Fiske. Cate couldn't imagine anyone wanting the original fancy breakfast she'd planned, but she raided the storerooms and pantry, came through with plates of fresh fruit, breads and preserves. Everyone said they weren't hungry, but both coffee and food disappeared every time she put out more.

Harm's men sprawled in the salon. Harm and Ivan kept charging in and out of the pilothouse. No one quit talking when Cate brought coffee or took away empty plates, so she heard everything that was going on.

Whatever anyone wanted to happen, a death on sea just wasn't exactly like a death on land. The captain had all the decision-making power onboard. It was his call to radio the coast guard, and when he discovered a CG cutter was less than two hours away, it was his decision to bring them in. Two ruddy-faced uniforms boarded just after ten.

In the meantime, she watched Harm's men, trying to imagine one of them harming Fiske, stealing that treasure of a formula. The three hung together, and pretty much never stopped talking about Fiske—it wasn't as if anyone could think about anything else—but nothing sounded odd to her.

"What else could it have been but a heart attack?" Arthur kept saying.

"It could have been a stroke," Yale kept saying right back.

"He liked his sweets. Didn't even try to keep the weight off," Purdue kept pointing out. "He must have had arteries clogged to the gills. And that's probably what he was doing in the middle of the night in the galley. Going after something to eat."

"Maybe we'll never know." Yale couldn't sit still, kept jumping up and pacing around the salon, staring at the sea, not seeing it. "But one way or another, I assume we'll immediately head home after this."

Cate suspected that going home was the ideal choice for the thief. Freedom of movement was easier in the home environment, where here, everyone was under Harm's microscope. The culprit could try playing the innocent card, but who could possibly do that 24/7 without a slipup?

Another hour of upheaval followed the coast guard's arrival. They met with Harm and Ivan, then took Fiske's body aboard their vessel and left. Moments after that, Ivan and Harm assembled the whole group in the salon to relay what would happen next.

Ivan started talking first. "Coast guard will be taking

Mr. Fiske to Juneau. There'll be an investigation started there, including an autopsy, no different than for any other unexplained death. That's pretty automatic before a body can be released out of state. For that matter, to you outlanders, I have to tell you, that'll probably take more time than the same basic investigation in the Lower 48."

"Which means what?" Arthur asked. "What kind of time are you talking about?"

"A week minimum is what they put on the table," Ivan said. "After that, Mr. Fiske'll be flown to Georgia, where I gather his daughter lives, the closest relative, so that's where the funeral will be held."

"Not by us, not in Cambridge?" Yale asked.

Harm stepped in then, and Ivan stepped back, poured himself a long, tall mug, braced it with whiskey, and heaved himself in a chair. Harm looked exhausted, Cate thought.

"No," Harm said. "It'll be with Fiske's daughter. I talked to her myself just a short time ago...."

Cate stopped listening for a few minutes, because she had heaps of dirty dishes and messes to clean up by then. And no one was thinking about lunch or dinner, but sooner or later they were both her responsibility. She needed to scour her galley. Think through what kind of foods might help calm down six traumatized men.

She'd just started a dishwasher load when she heard voices raised, grabbed a towel to dry her hands and walked back into the salon—at least as far as the doorway. The stress in the air was combustible. Ivan and Hans had disappeared back to the pilothouse, clearly to let Harm deal with his men.

"We don't have a choice," Harm was saying. Purdue and Yale were hunched over, like sprinters ready to race flat out. The older Arthur was the one whose harsh voice rasped in the air.

"It's just wrong. Being here. Everything's wrong."

"I know, Arthur. I feel the same. None of us are going to be in vacation mode after this. But the coast guard wants us to stay here for the next week."

"I still don't get it," Purdue snapped. "Fiske had a heart attack. Or whatever. It had nothing to do with us. You'd think we were under suspicion."

Cate wiped her hands harder, realizing the sudden silence was an answer in itself. They all felt under suspicion—for the theft in the company. But now Fiske's death had a question mark about it, as well.

"The coast guard is the authority in these waters. They want us on the boat where we're all easy to find, easy to question. There's nothing any of us can do for Fiske's family—or anything else—until the investigation is done. Cause of death has to be determined."

"I understand that," Arthur said. "But I don't see why that has anything to do with any of us."

Since Harm had clearly already answered that, he pushed on. "Ivan has agreed that he'll sail us back to Juneau as soon as we get the okay from the authorities. Otherwise, we keep on the original time schedule. I'll be in daily contact with the authorities. If there's any way to get this resolved sooner, Ivan will speed up our return to base. Also…speaking for myself, I wouldn't want to fly back to the mainland and home, knowing Fiske was still in Juneau, with no resolution for him."

There, Cate thought. Harm had found the one thing they could all agree on. None of the men wanted to leave Alaska until Fiske did.

"So that's it for now," Harm said.

That might have been "it", but Cate watched the day deteriorate from disaster to major gloom. Once the coast guard cutter disappeared from sight, all of them—except for Ivan—wandered around the yacht like lost souls. No one wanted food. No one wanted to talk. No one wanted to sit. No one could settle down or rest or sleep.

Cate couldn't fathom how anything could make the situation better...until the whales showed up.

Harm's ears were ringing. He'd been stuck in the pilothouse for hours because his cell phone connection kept petering out, and the only other means of communicating to the outside was the radio. Ivan and Hans showed him how to work it. Since then, he'd been on it nonstop. There seemed no end to what needed to be communicated—calls to the company, calls to Fiske's daughter in Georgia, calls to the firm's attorneys, calls to the P.I. firm he'd been working with.

Cate kept popping into the pilothouse, delivering coffee and food, taking away remnants from the last batch. She was...extraordinary. Yesterday he'd thought she was full of herself...and he knew damn well she had reason to be "full of herself" after sampling that woman's dangerous kisses.

But today, in a crisis, she'd just stepped up the way...

well, hell. The same way he did. No conversation. Just filling in where something needed doing, taking charge without asking or making any fanfare about it. She'd taken better care of his men than their mothers likely would have—all with that sexy butt and godforsaken hairstyle, and now that he realized it, those deep, soft eyes of hers.

"Harm." Ivan had given up calling him "Mr. Connolly" the instant they'd stood over a dead body together. Still, the captain's voice maintained a deferential tone. "There's another message coming in."

Ivan shifted so that Harm could stand in front of the ship's receiving device. Few electronics worked this far from the mainland except for the ship's equipment, Harm was discovering. And the message just coming in put a burr in his pulse.

"Problem?" Ivan asked. Yet before waiting for an answer, he suddenly glanced out the window, promptly cut the engines, and swiftly motioned for Harm to look out.

Harm stepped around Ivan. His jaw dropped when he saw the strange, huge mounds in the sea moving toward the boat. "Those can't be whales," he said.

"Oh, yeah, they are."

For the first time that day—maybe for the first time in weeks—Harm felt something quiet in his soul. Beyond the sea in every direction were mountainous islands, cliffs and ragged slopes that speared the sky. Fragrant pines somehow found purchase in the rock, adding a rich spice to the air, a verdant green against the pale sky. On almost every turn of land there was an eagle—or a nest of them—overlooking its regal domain.

The "mounds" in the sea, though, were something else. Hans had already opened the pilothouse door, directed by Ivan to urge everyone topside.

"They're humpbacks," Ivan told Harm. "Looks like an extraordinary sized pod from here. I can count… twelve? Thirteen?"

Temporarily, Harm couldn't breathe. The whales were giants. From a distance, each one looked bigger than the yacht, and the whole group of them—or pod—was swimming straight for the boat.

"You cut the engines?" Harm asked, trying to comprehend why they weren't sailing full bore in the opposite direction.

"Yeah. We're in their territory. Good chance for everyone to see 'em up close."

The pilothouse was only three steps above the foredeck, so Harm immediately saw when Purdue hustled to the rails, then Arthur, Yale and Cate charging behind him. For the first moment since hearing of Fiske's death, the group was diverted from their dark mood. But it was Cate that Harm's gaze homed on… honed on.

She burst out of the galley, saw the whales and made a delighted sound of laughter. "Aren't they gorgeous?" she demanded of his boys.

"Why are they still coming so close?" Harm asked.

"I suspect…because they're curious about us. It's not as if they're afraid. Those behemoths haven't experienced anything they need to be afraid of."

Curious? Everywhere, these big hunks arched out of the sea, aiming straight for the yacht, parting to surround it, half going on one side, half on the other. Harm figured any second this was going to turn into a Jonah-gobbled-by-the-whale day…and there below was Cate, leaning so far over the rail it was a miracle she didn't fall in, still laughing, fearless, delighted.

And then he realized she was really leaning over. Her whole body was leaning over.

He reacted by instinct, pushing past Ivan, taking the steps down from the pilothouse in a single leap. She was going to fall. He knew it. He could see it. The least tip, and she'd tumble into that icy water.

Instead of helping her, his three men and Hans, stood like statues against the rail. They were all staring at Cate with a look of shock. It took a heart-thrashing second for Harm to realize what she was actually doing.

She was leaning so far out, with her arm fully extended…

To pet a whale.

The big guy, swimming alongside the boat, suddenly berthed in a smooth arch—close enough to the boat to bump it. In fact, he did bump it. The men all felt it.

And they all heard Cate's giggle of delight, as if she'd just taught a puppy a new trick.

The whale circled, blew a fountain from his blowhole and dipped beneath the surface again. Harm hoped he'd disappear, go off wherever whales went off to, but instead the huge thing surfaced again. This time it surfaced beneath Cate's hand. Apparently, it was coming back for another petting.

Harm heard her murmuring love words, crooning. To the whale, for Pete's sake—who bumped the boat again in response.

But he also saw her face. Her expression was as simple and complex as joy. Damn, but she was fearless. Open to embracing anything. When had he last felt that free, that excited about the possibilities?

"Hey, Cate." Ivan showed up from above. "Did anyone ever mention that you didn't have the brain God gave a goose?"

Cate didn't even lift her head. "He's so beautiful. I thought he'd be cold. And the surface of his body was cold, but beneath, there's this…thundering warmth. He's smooth and even soft—"

"Y'all want to take a vote on whether she's certifiable?" Ivan rolled his eyes with the guys.

"That's it, make fun." Cate scowled at the lot of them, then cast one more longing glance as the big behemoth swam off to his pals.

"Gonna take him home, Cate? Got a big enough bathtub for him, do you?"

"I'd like to see you bring home a date. Bet his eyes'd pop when he saw your choice of pets."

"You like your boys big, do you?" That brought on a round of raucous laughter.

"Size does matter, boys," Cate said demurely, and that brought another round of hoots and laughter.

She caught his eye moments later. There was just a flash in hers, a connection, but he got it. It wasn't a day for laughter—just a day when they all needed some kind of comic relief. Cate had willingly provided it.

But when she looked at him, he knew she hadn't forgotten finding Fiske in her galley. And his mind kept replaying how she'd behaved with that damned whale. So fearless. Reaching out to something she should have known was seriously dangerous.

And that wasn't just whales and thieves.

It was him, too.

Harm spun around, told himself to quit obsessing on those haunting kisses and those sassy eyes and forget her. The message waiting for him in the pilothouse had come from the P.I. firm he hired in Cambridge. More troubling news. Bad news. A mounting trail of evidence defining a very clever thief.

But nothing to identify him.

And there was no way Harm could keep Cate safe—or any of his other men—until he somehow found that answer. Fast.

Chapter 5

The instant the boat docked at Tennehee Springs late that afternoon, the men charged off as if their feet were spring-loaded.

"You get the feeling the whole group needs a little stress relief?" Cate murmured to Harm.

They were bringing up the rear. He naturally cupped her arm when she took the leap to the dock. She felt the bolt of awareness—so did he, judging from the wry glance he shot her. Still, they followed the others, walking side by side.

"We all might need a few hours' rest, but we're not the only ones. Cate, you're funnier than hell and full of the devil. I really want to say—thanks."

"Thanks for what?" she asked in surprise.

"For taking care of trouble. Which you've been doing solid since we all got onboard. You didn't sign on for these kinds of problems…much less for the trauma of finding Fiske. For someone who could use some sympathy, you're not getting any, but you're damned good at giving it out."

"You've completely misunderstood," she assured him. "I don't know any of you, so don't give me credit for sensitivity. I'm not one of those touchy-feely caretaking kind of women."

"Ah."

"I'm not."

"Okay, slugger. I'm sorry I said something nice about you. I'll try not to do it again."

She considered punching him, figured that likely a rich hotshot like him hadn't been punched in a good long time—but she didn't. She was far too mature, she told herself righteously. Besides, she couldn't very well fight with him and stick closer than glue for this outing. Just because she wasn't a maternal or nurturing type didn't mean she couldn't feel sympathy. Harm had had a god-awful morning. A god-awful month, it sounded like. And he was the lone ranger, stuck with all the repercussions.

"Hey," Ivan yelled from the leader dog role in the head of the straggly line. "If anyone strays off the road, that's fine. Go walkabout wherever you want. It's not as if anyone could get lost here. We're here three hours, then back to the ship."

"As if anyone needed those instructions," Cate said drily, but she was as taken by Tennehee Springs as Harm seemed to be. Just the exercise of walking in the brisk air seemed to shake off the gloomy mood on the boat, and the unexpectedly different world offshore seemed to capture all their attentions.

From the dock—where a hefty number of fishing vessels were already tied off—began an ambling gravel road. She never saw or heard a car, although mud-covered ATVs were parked here and there. The houses lining the road looked more like cottages than structures that could regularly survive an Alaskan winter. Cats and dogs snoozed on every porch step. "Incredibly majestic woods and hills, and then screen doors with holes," Harm said.

It was a contrast. Eventually, they came to a café—Ivan's goal was to get the local flavor of a drink and dinner here. Next door, a hand-painted sign read: Is There Life After Death? Trespass Here And Find Out.

And at the door to the café was another sign—Leave Guns Outside. Clearly, the customers were into obeying, because a whole teepee of rifles and long guns were perched against the window. Cate couldn't believe the number, and when she stepped inside ahead of Harm, she couldn't believe the place.

"Holy kamoly. We're sure not in Kansas anymore, Toto," Cate mentioned, making Harm smile—for the first time all day.

"We're supposed to eat dinner here, huh?"

"Yup. I get a night off whenever we're onshore. More to the point, I do believe I'll be able to serve you guys anything after this and you'll love it."

She almost ran into Yale and Purdue, who'd stopped dead to gape for a moment when they walked in, too. The café was decorated early-box. All supplies were in boxes, unstacked and unopened until needed. A splash of rickety tables took up the rest of the space. A swinging blackboard announced the cook's menu for the day—which was chili, either hot as hell or the sissy version. Another sign forbade spitting on the floor.

The group filed around the big round table in the corner. Cate gingerly took a seat between Harm and Ivan and mentally lectured herself against galloping into the kitchen to find a rag and soap and some way to scour the table. For darn sure, it hadn't been washed in recent history. On the other hand, an exuberantly friendly lady with a mighty chest and rambunctious smile immediately came over to take their liquor order.

Beer was the poison of choice. The waitress/owner put enough longnecks in the center of the table to last three weeks and then some, Cate thought. Initially, their table was silent. Listening to the chatter between the other customers was more engrossing than anything they could possibly say. The longest discussion involved a "little" domestic abuse the week before that included a fire, blown-out windows, screaming matches and the husband finally giving up and calling in the law.

Apparently, calling in the law meant that someone literally had to either boat or fly in, because there wasn't any law here. Once the chili was served—Cate chose the hell-hot version—Ivan said to Harm, "You beginning to get it?"

"Get what?" Harm asked.

"The complications of your man dying here. This just isn't like the Lower 48. No place is more beautiful than here. No better place to be independent, be your own man, make your own way. But trying to get bureaucratic things done on a fast timetable—it just doesn't happen."

"Different values here," Harm said.

"Ask me, they're better values. But I'm sure I'd feel different if I had an employee die on my watch, and had all your kind of responsibilities."

Harm didn't respond—but then everyone was guzzling beer in gulping heaps by then. The chili was *that* hot. Locals eventually left until only one other table was occupied, filled by a pair of hunched-over bearded men who were stargazing into their beer. Cate wasn't about to touch Harm, but someone should. Where the others loosened up after the food and alcohol, he sat tough and dark-eyed, obviously unable to relax with the weight of monster-size problems on his shoulders.

When the smoke from the chili cleared, Yale put down his beer, which was probably his fourth. "Something just occurred to me. We're all gonna know."

"You're slurring your words," Arthur said impatiently. "We're all going to know what?"

"We got a thief in our company," Yale told Ivan brazenly. "Somebody took a formula. Worth millions. Maybe billions. Maybe worth nothing, too, because the data disappeared…but that's just what occurred to me. The data's gonna reshow up. In someone else's company. Then whoever sold us out is gonna be very, very rich. And then we'll know who it really was."

"You're drunk, Yale." Purdue moved his colleague's beer away. "This isn't anybody's business but ours."

"But that's the thing, you see? What would be the

point of anyone stealing if they didn't get rich from it? But the minute the money shows up, the minute somebody gets rich, then we'll know who it is."

Cate saw the men all looking at Harm, as if they all expected him to put a lid on Yale—to stop the whole conversation. Instead, he eased back in his chair, and she remembered what he'd said—that he'd brought his team on this trip, to a place where they'd be isolated, out of their normal realm. He wanted to see if his staff could, or would, unravel—so he could discover what happened if they did.

When no one picked up Yale's conversational lead, he reached over the table and grabbed another longneck. "The thing that really messes with my head," he said, "is that all this time, I thought it was Fiske. You know. Because it had to be the financial guy, because it's always the financial guys who know how much money is really involved—and who know how to get to it."

"I don't see how it could ever have been Fiske," Purdue said. "Fiske had a heart of gold."

"So do whores, they say."

"Watch your mouth," Arthur scolded, but then quietly, "I think anyone can be tempted to do anything…if the stakes are high enough."

"And maybe the stakes weren't money. Maybe it was something more important than money," Purdue offered.

"That's stupid. There's nothing more important than money—at least when it's big money." Yale sighed, then let out a gigantic hiccup. "The thing is, if it was Fiske, then it's almost the worst thing. Because the money might never show up. The formula might never show up. We not only won't have the money or the data, but the world won't have the damned cure. We'll all be under a cloud of suspicion forever. You still suspicion us all, don't you, Harm?"

"*Suspicion* isn't a verb," Purdue said with disgust, and hauled him to his feet. "That's why I went to Purdue and you went to Yale. I wanted an education. You never got one. You don't even know what you're saying." To the others, "I'm taking him back to the boat. Although I might have to roll him there."

"I'll go, too." Hans stood, followed by Ivan. All of them ended up hiking back at the same time. As if reflecting the group's mood, the clouds bunched up and produced another version of Alaska's "summer rain"—drenching them in a downpour as they climbed aboard.

Cate retreated to the galley, where she cleaned and fussed and rearranged—and then did it all over again. Over the next hour, voices and sounds gradually faded away. She assumed everyone had caved below deck, needing rest after the long day, but there was no chance of her sleeping yet. She wandered through the empty salon, pushed open the doors to the aft deck. The deluge had stopped, the skies were just barely dripping, and the lightning had faded to a luminescent pearl-gray.

Her pulse jolted when she saw Harm, leaning over the rail. The shadowed overhang concealed his expression, but his posture was both tense and exhausted. He was staring at the black-silver waters as if his worries were as impossibly deep as those seas.

Before Harm realized she was there, Cate figured she should back up and back off, head below. It was easy to guess he didn't want company—much less hers.

Since she never seemed to make the wisest choices, she edged closer instead. She didn't say anything, just leaned over the rail right next to him. She felt his startled stiffening. Ignored it. He was as alone as a man could be, had no one to turn to. Maybe that wasn't her problem... but she was the only one who seemed to be able to do something about it.

"I'm not good company right now," he said.

He didn't say go away, but he might as well have. "I can't imagine you would be. After everything that happened today, I figured you might be in a mood to kick someone around. I'm not a bad kickee. You don't owe me anything. I'm not in your company radar. And I'm tough as nails."

"You're not remotely tough as nails. And quit looking at me that way."

"What way?"

He turned, just far enough so she could see his glower. "You think I won't bite your head off—I will."

"Go for it," she urged him. "Bite."

The conversation didn't make much sense, but when he suddenly grabbed her...that made sense, she thought. He was pretty angry. Not at her, but at life. And at himself, she suspected, because he couldn't solve unsolvable problems and find answers out of thin air—which he apparently expected himself to do.

So his hands were rough on her shoulders. He yanked her closer. His mouth slapped on hers, communicating pressure and dominance, and probably he intended to arouse fear in her. He was one pissed-off kahuna, all right.

Still, she didn't back off and she didn't kick back. She did what any other lunatic of a woman would do.

She melted. Right into him. Closing her eyes, feeling herself going soft and pliant all over. Feeling the rush of sensation when his kiss darkened, deepened, took.

Thrilling. Hells bells, it was a word out of her grandmother's time, out of old movies in the forties in black-and-white. Real women weren't thrilled by a guy's kisses today. The whole idea was romantic and stupid.

Yet thrills kept shivering through her bloodstream, making her heart pound, making her knees feel weak. Making need shoot through her body with cat claws, sharp and real. It was just desire, she told herself. Nothing important. Just hormones.

But it didn't feel like "just hormones." His mouth felt like an answer to a question she'd never asked, the taste of him a spice and flavor she'd never known, the heat and power of him something her heart had craved her whole life—even if she'd never known it.

Her hands walked around him, closing around his waist, inviting the glue of his brick-hard chest against her soft breasts, his tense abdomen against her cushioning pelvis. Oh, yeah, she thought. This was worth dying for. Who knew?

When he suddenly jerked his head up, she just might have fallen if he wasn't still holding on to her. She had to intake a good gulp of air, and even then, her head still felt foggy. His expression, she noted, was still glowering.

But the anxiety and exhaustion and world of worry was gone. He was still mad.

But now, he was only mad at her.

"My God, you're trouble," he grumped.

"Watch it. Compliments go straight to my head."

There. After that whole impossibly terrible day, she got a real smile out of him. Not that half-eaten grin he'd unwillingly let through in the café, but a real chuckle, a sign he'd thrown off a pound of that unbearable heaviness he'd been carrying around. But he removed his hands from her shoulders as if suddenly realizing his palms had been cooking on a hot stove, and immediately leaned back against the rail.

"I was married twice," he said abruptly.

Now there was a conversation starter. "Yeah? That's good."

His eyebrows shot up. "Good? Most women run like hell when they hear that."

She suspected they did. She suspected that was exactly why he'd mentioned that little bit of biographical information out of the blue. "My theory is that pretty much all men run from commitment after they've been burned twice. Even if they were to blame for doing a good share of the burning. Divorces are no fun for either side, or so I hear. Anyway, I appreciate your telling me. Now I know you're safe."

"Safe." He rolled the word on his tongue, as if he'd never heard anyone, much less a woman, call him *safe*.

"Hey, I'm footloose. Not looking for a commitment.

So it wouldn't do for me to fall in love or you to fall in love with me. I don't like hurting people—or being hurt. And you know what, Harm? I think you've been hurt enough."

"You don't know that."

"I know you kiss like you mean it. That's all I have to know." She pushed off the railing. "The next time, though..."

He rolled his eyes. "I hear the warning in your voice. The next time, what?"

"The next time, don't start something you don't intend to finish."

There now, she'd shocked him again. She walked away, thinking she'd done what she wanted to do— which was remove that exhaustion and stress from his face for a few minutes.

Of course, she'd also the same as dared him to make love to her.

As she locked the door to her cabin, already chafing at the claustrophobic space, she told herself it was about time she learned to curb her impulsive tongue. But the internal scolding didn't last after she turned off the light. Yeah, she'd dared him. Yeah, it was a foolish and risky thing to suggest to a man of his power and virility, with a life so alien to hers.

But she didn't regret it. She figured she should. That maybe she could talk herself into believing she didn't want to make love with him. But her heart...just didn't seem to swallow that good sense.

* * *

The next morning, when Cate heard the first sounds of voices in the dining room, she poked her head around the galley archway. "Just pour yourself some coffee, guys. And start with the fruit. I'll be bringing in breakfast in two shakes."

Her galley, she knew, looked as if a cyclone had hit. Outside, a blazing sun seemed to wash away all the gloom and troubles from yesterday—which unfortunately didn't improve her own mood. She hadn't slept well.

As anyone with a brain knew, mess with the cook's sleep and everybody paid. She was grumpier than a porcupine with a tummy ache.

"One-minute warning. Y'all better be sitting down," she called out. The Ebelskivers pan on the stovetop was hers. It took a unique pan to create the dish. The recipe for Danish pancakes was lighter than air, each one filled with a treat—like blueberries or cherries or a little orange marmalade or a scoop of wild honey. A few she filled with ham and cheese to make them more substantial. The boys could pick them up with their hands if they wanted. They didn't even have to use silverware.

"Need help?"

There. Her heart slammed like mad out of the complete blue, even before she whirled around and saw Harm. The circles under his eyes were bigger than whales, a testimony that he hadn't slept any better than she had. But when a man looked that rough around the edges, how could he still exude so much virility and sexiness?

"No," she said with no fanfare and no apology. As she'd reminded herself fifty million times in the middle of the night, she barely knew the man.

So she'd made a major judgment mistake and tried him. No one could be hopelessly addicted that fast. No one. "Out," she said, and immediately turned around.

It wasn't tricky to make Ebelskivers. It was just tricky to make them exquisitely perfect, and Cate wanted them better than even exquisite. When she had a free second—and she only had a single free second because the Ebelskivers couldn't be left—she dashed into the dining room and put a glazed flowerpot of monkey bread on the table.

"You just pull it apart with your hands, guys. Eat it like that. The Ebelskivers are on their way in, but I've only got one pan, so they have to come out in shifts."

She'd just dashed back into the galley when Ivan showed up. "Out," she said.

At least he knew enough to obey by now.

They started diving in. She heard the first round of marriage proposals and vows of eternal love while she plopped in the second batch. In spite of the blinding sun, a stiff wind seemed determined to push the boat around. Since the stove was perfectly gimballed, the surface was automatically made level—and it wasn't as if she hadn't cooked in far worse conditions than this—but the pitch and roll still made cooking a wee bit more challenging.

She ran in with the next batch. By then, the men were hovering over the table, looking like kin to pigs at a trough. No one was drooling, but they'd all turned into obedient children—no hair combed, no shaved chins, but all with the same expressions.

"Each of you has that angelic look men get when they want sex. I'm not fooled," she said. "And you can't have sweets and carbohydrates like this all the time, so don't beg."

"We just want you to cook forever for us, Cate."

Harm said, "Have you had even a bite?"

Actually, she hadn't. Who had time? She'd share coffee with them when the last batch was done and on the table. For now, she had one more platter to go...and she was thinking, really, it wasn't like today could be good for any of them. Fiske's death was still fresh. So maybe she'd put together another round of comfort foods later. Like strawberry pie? Fresh? And maybe one more batch of peppermint cookies.

She opened the cupboard, watching her Ebelskivers, glanced in to check her spices, reached for the peppermint extract...and stopped dead.

The peppermint extract bottle had no top.

In her lifetime, Cate had never put away a spice without securing the lid. Spices aged too fast as it was.

Confused, she reached for the small container, and stopped dead again. The bottle was completely empty.

It couldn't be. True peppermint extract was so strong that she never used more than a drop at a time. And she'd just opened it days before to make the first batch of her original cookies. The bottle should have been full, just short a couple of drops. She'd bought fresh from her favorite supplier before the trip.

"Cate?"

A sudden vision of Fiske filled her mind. The way he'd been lying on the galley floor, the oddness of his hands cupped around his neck as if he'd been choking.

A wisp of smoke startled her, made her realize her pancakes were burning. She grabbed the handle, saved the cakes in the nick of time, scooped that last round onto a plate and carted them into the dining room.

At a glance, she could see the men were filling up. Hands were going on tummies. The guys were getting that glazed-eye look testifying that they'd been sugared-up and filled-up for now...except for Harm.

His gaze found hers across the table, shrewd and sharp as one of her Wüsthof-Trident knives. "You all right?"

"Sure," she said. But she wasn't. She wasn't remotely all right. She wasn't sure if she was ever going to be all right again. Maybe it was crazy—she had to hope she was crazy—but the thought in her mind was as indelible as lead ink. Fiske had been murdered. And not just murdered, but killed by someone on the boat.

Once she set down the platter, she poured herself a mug of coffee and held it with both hands so she could keep the darned thing from shaking as she sat down. She was sitting with a murderer, her mind kept telling her—which was probably why her heart was pounding louder than a freight train.

The craziest thing of all was that she was the only one who knew what had happened. And even if she told, she couldn't imagine anyone would believe her.

Chapter 6

Immediately after breakfast, Harm joined Ivan in the pilothouse, where he could use the radio to check with Juneau. The response didn't take long. Harm made a sound of irritation as he clicked off.

Ivan said, "What?"

"In the immortal words of the authorities, the pathologist is fishing."

"Ah. This is Alaska," Ivan said, as if that was an answer in itself.

"He'll get to the autopsy. But maybe not today. Or tomorrow. *Soon,* I believe, was the word used by the office."

Ivan said, "It's just different thinking up here. The man's dead, so what's the hurry?"

"That we've all been put in limbo until we have results from the tests? That the man has a daughter who very likely wants to plan a funeral?" Harm shook his head again. "I'm going below. The coroner asked me to go through Fiske's things. The coast guard took the list of his medical conditions and medicines, but they want me to check to see if there were any other medicines or things he might have been taking that weren't on the list."

"You want me to ask Hans to do it?" Ivan asked.

"No. I'm fine." Harm clipped below deck, hoping to catch Cate en route, but she wasn't in the galley or the dining area. Something had shaken her at breakfast. Since nothing seemed to shake Cate—certainly not whales or finding dead guys—Harm figured it must have been something substantial.

Not that she was any of his business…but sweet damn, she'd become his business. The dimensions of the why and how, right then, he refused to examine.

First off, anyway, he needed to explore Fiske's belongings. No one was below deck. The men were all topside for the sail toward Baranof and Hot Springs— their next land destination. Fiske's cabin was big enough for a squirrel. Fiske's duffel was sitting navy-tight on his bunk.

Harm rifled through it, found four brown plastic prescription containers. One was a statin, a cholesterol drug Harm recognized. Two were heart medicines, and the last—he just didn't know. Never heard of the name, and the labeling didn't indicate what the one-a-day dosage was for. All the medicines had already been reported to the coast guard.

Harm hefted the heart pills, feeling a sharp gulp.

Yesterday, the coast guard had come to the most obvious conclusion—that Fiske was an overweight guy under a lot of stress, a heart attack or stroke waiting to happen. Harm hadn't created that stress, but he still felt responsible for failing to find answers that could have alleviated it. Fiske was a good soul. His uncle's closest friend in the company.

Harm bent over, hoping to find something else in Fiske's belongings. He saw the corner of an old, battered red-leather case—just a calendar—and was about to pull it out when he heard Cate.

"Harm?"

He didn't have to spin around and see her face to know something was wrong. It was like at breakfast. Her usual sass and sparkle had disappeared. There was none of the full-of-herself sexy love of the night before, the daredevil, the troublemaker. Just a quiet voice and nerves. "I need to tell you something," she said. "And you're not going to believe me."

"Why wouldn't I believe you?"

"Because no one will. No one's going to take this seriously. And you won't, either. Trust me."

"I do trust you." Quickly, he steered her out of Fiske's cabin, out of the empty corridor and into his cabin. Last night, after she'd damned near seduced him—and thoroughly rattled his timbers—he'd vowed not to be in private quarters with her alone unless…well, unless.

This definitely wasn't an "unless." But he could tell from her face that he wouldn't want anyone else hearing this—or even knowing that she was talking privately with him.

"It's about Fiske," she said. She obviously couldn't stand still. She started pacing—and promptly bumped into his chest the first time she did a spin around. "I think someone killed him, Harm. With peppermint."

"Say what?"

"I know. Death by peppermint. It sounds silly. Crazy. Impossible. And part of the problem is that I don't think anyone would know. How could authorities think of this? Why would a pathologist test for it? He wouldn't. It's not a drug."

"Whoa. Start at the beginning. I'm having trouble following." He didn't push her on the bed, just framed his hands around her shoulders and gently sat her down. Two of them couldn't pace at the same time. And once she'd suggested murder, Harm figured he had the biggest reason to pace.

He heard her spill out the details. The empty peppermint bottle. The missing lid. The way she'd found Fiske, his position indicating he'd been clawing at his neck, as if he were choking. But there'd been no sign of vomit. And the bottle had been put away, except for the lid.

"Do you understand, Harm? I don't see anyone will find evidence of it in an autopsy because it's not a drug or anything anyone would ever test for you. But I would think it would create a burning in the esophagus or throat. You could ask them that, couldn't you? To look for it?"

"Yes. I'll radio immediately on this."

"That's why I had to tell you. Because if you don't ask, I don't see how they'd find it."

"But I'm still not totally grasping this, Cate. I mean, peppermint's a candy. And you made cookies from it. And I think I remember a grandmother advising that you could rub it on a sore tooth. Couldn't it have been like that? He got a toothache, got up in the middle of the night, thought he'd try that old wives' tale, and that's how he got into your peppermint?"

"No. I mean, yes, it's possible he had a toothache, might have known of that old wives' tale. But if that were the case, he'd have used a drop or two, not the whole bottle. No one would take a whole bottle of peppermint by choice. It couldn't happen. Your throat would burn like fire. You might try it by accident, not realizing that…but then you'd rush to a sink, to the nearest water, start spitting it out, do anything to make it stop burning."

Harm spun around, only to find that Cate had bounced up from the bed and was trying to pace again, too. It couldn't happen. Not in a space the size of an animal cage.

"Maybe he dropped the bottle. Spilled it. And that's why it was empty. It seems logical to me that he'd have thought peppermint would soothe his stomach, something like that. You know he ate like a horse that night, easy to believe he had a stomachache—"

"That could have been. And I'm not trying to say that I know how he died. For that matter, maybe he did die of a heart attack. If someone forced him to intake a whole bottle of peppermint, I can well believe it caused an impossible shock to his heart. I'm not a doctor. Just a chef. And I'm telling you…someone handled my peppermint in a way that couldn't have been an accident. Someone used the entire bottle. Someone, not me, didn't put the lid back on. And if Fiske had been the one to think he wanted it, who touched it, then swallowed that amount, there's no way in the universe he'd have been physically capable of putting it back in the cupboard and closing the door and leaving the galley all tidy. He'd have been frantic to stop the burning in his mouth and throat."

"Okay. I hear you. I got it. But who knows that stuff about peppermint?"

She thought about that, answered slowly, "I have no idea. I mean, I'd think it would be common knowledge from someone like me, a chef, a cook, someone who knows foods. But otherwise…well, I can't imagine why you'd know it. Or any other normal person. I guess I'd assume a scientist-type might, just because they'd get the chemistry part of it."

Unfortunately, all his men had that background—that is, everyone but him. His mind kept replaying the men, the dignified Arthur, the Ivy-League boys with their arrogance and outward devotion to their jobs and the cancer cause.

"I just can't figure out the why. If there was a murder, it was logically to cover up the theft. Only there's no sane reason for the theft." He socked a fist into the other hand. "If greed were the motivation, I'd get it. Power, I'd get it. But neither of those make sense. The man was already going to get money—big money—when the medicine hit the market. He was already going to be part of the massive credit, the satisfaction, for finding a cure for this uniquely destructive cancer. So why steal it? Why try selling it elsewhere, where the instant the sale came to light, the thief would be identified? None of it makes any sense."

"Harm?"

"What?"

"Sit down. Calm down."

Nobody told him to sit down and calm down. Ever. He sat down. Calmed down.

"You're taking me seriously," she said quietly, as if she were still having trouble believing it.

"Of course. Why wouldn't I?"

"Because it's not going to sound credible to anyone. Death by peppermint? You know it sounds silly."

"Yeah, it does. In fact, it sounds so downright ridiculous that I can't imagine why the two of us aren't laughing our heads off."

He watched her take in a massive breath. The way she looked at him. He couldn't read it, but there was something there. Something both warm and wary, as if he'd done something that mattered to her.

"You know," she said quietly, "I didn't expect to like you. It's awkward."

"Your liking another human being is awkward?"

"You joke. But you feel it, too. We're going to have to watch it," she said gently.

"Watch what?"

"Harm. Don't be obtuse. There's something really, really weird happening here."

"You're telling me? Murder, theft—"

"Those are just…problems. The weird thing I mean is

between you and me." She leaned over, close enough to kiss him. He thought she was going to. Her lips parted. Her eyes seemed to darken. She was so close he could smell her sweet skin, feel her warm breath, see her impossibly soft lips. "Don't you tempt me, Connolly. I can't possibly belong in your life. You can't possibly imagine me in yours. So you just quit it."

My God, the woman was batty. She told him she was going up to talk to the captain and left. Harm was willing to admit he was feeling on the batty side himself. His key financial guy murdered? He needed to head upstairs, radio Juneau, somehow ask for the pathologist to make sure they examined Fiske's throat and esophagus without sounding like a nutcase. This whole mess just kept getting worse.

And Cate was somehow… He didn't know what she was doing. Implying they were a pair in some way. Implying they were in this together somehow. Implying they had some kind of kindred spirit, man-woman, serious connection going on.

Implying he knew it.

The real helluva a thing was…he *did* know it. Not that he'd admit it to her. Hell, he wasn't remotely ready to admit it to himself.

Cate jumped when she heard a footstep behind her… but it was just Ivan, popping in the galley for a raid on the first-aid kit. "Connolly's up in the pilothouse, calling in authorities again. I don't know whether this is turning into the trip from hell or a hell of an interesting cruise. But I'm taking an ibuprofen while I'm deciding."

He shook a couple pills from the container. Cate handed him a cup of water. "I was hoping to catch you alone for a minute or two."

"Honey, I've been trying to catch you alone since I hired you on."

For once, Cate wasn't annoyed by his flirting. At least it was normal, and right now, anything normal had an incredible appeal. "I just think I should tell you something, Ivan."

"Oh, good. Anything of an intimate or personal nature would be preferable." Ivan set the cup back on the counter after he'd downed the pills, shot her a lascivious grin.

She ignored it. "I think Fiske died from peppermint."

"Huh?"

She expected the comical expression on his face. Still, she showed him the vial of peppermint, how it had been left, all the things she'd told Harm. Only Ivan responded by cocking his hands on his hips and letting out a good belly laugh.

"Cate, you doofus, we all had tons of your peppermint cookies the first night out—"

"You don't understand. This isn't peppermint, as in the dose that goes into candy or cookies or baking. It's the whole—" But abruptly she stopped talking when she saw Yale leaning in the doorway.

"I apologize. I didn't want to interrupt a serious conversation. But I was up on deck. Hans came out of the pilothouse, asked if I'd mind seeing if you were in the galley, said to tell you there was salmon." Yale gave a boyish shrug, as if to say he knew the message didn't make sense.

Apparently, it did to Ivan, though. Cate heard the boat engine suddenly slow, then the boat changed direction and circled, then stopped. Ivan turned to her with an exuberant grin. "So there'll be a delay before reaching Baranof Springs, my gorgeous, adorable chef, for a spot of fishing. Is there a prayer you could alter the dinner menu to do a little something with fresh salmon?"

Murders and mayhem and poison by peppermint aside, Cate gave him the rhetorical answer. "Is the Pope Catholic? Is a rabbi Jewish? You get me fresh salmon, I'll give you nectar."

"Attagirl."

Because she was too distracted to duck, the captain managed to squeeze her behind before she could elbow him away. Yale scratched his whiskery chin, looking as innocent as a child. "Did I accidentally sabotage a private conversation?"

"No, not at all," she said, but she was rattled times ten. She hadn't expected Ivan to take her seriously, to believe her. But she still wished no one had overheard. There was enough worry and suspicion floating around the boat without someone being in a position to add fuel to it…not even counting that Yale was one of the three who could have been the thief—and murderer.

A shiver chased up her spine. Cate, her sisters always said, was the fearless one. Nothing shook her. Nothing made her back down. She always raced ahead as if she had nothing to lose.

But that was the thing. All her life, she'd really never felt she did have anything to lose.

But Harm did. And out of the blue, she seemed hopelessly connected to a man who should have been, and by any definition still was, a relative stranger. And risk suddenly had a different flavor. The flavor of fear.

Four hours later she heard the men laughing in the dining room. "Don't get near Cate. You should see that knife she's got."

"I don't need knives to make you men behave," Cate called out and then showed up in the doorway with the first platter. She was still wearing her old Kmart jacket with the tear, the same frayed sweatshirt underneath, while the guys had just pushed off their fancy-dancy rain outfits. Rain hadn't stopped any of them from fishing, though, not once the first salmon was reeled in.

"Under the salmon is an Agrodolce sauce, boys. Nothing to scare you, trust me." True fresh salmon— Alaskan salmon—didn't need any fancying up, but she couldn't resist the bed of Agrodolce sauce to pretty it up. The salmon itself just had the slightest sprinkling of butcher's salt and fresh pepper. She carted the individual platters to each man. For the extras, she added a plate of Georgian cheese bread, a bowl of zucchini ribbons— just barely sprinkled with tarragon—and then plain old baked potatoes.

For over twenty minutes, there wasn't a word. She glanced at Harm now and then. He glanced right back. She hadn't regained any sense of safety since that morning, but damnation. Watching the guys fish—it had all been so normal. Yelling at each other, screaming when they got a fighter on the line, Ivan netting their loot, her laying claim to the booty for dinner. And now. The way they gobbled up the food like children raised in caves, hooking their arms around their plates as if fearful of interlopers, shoveling it down, making orgasmic sounds right at the table.

After a while, she just cupped her chin in a hand and watched. Killers? How can any of them possibly be killers?

"This isn't really salmon," Arthur said at one point. "I don't care for fish, to tell you the truth."

"Alaskan fish aren't like anything you get in the Lower 48," Ivan explained.

"It's the cold waters. Cold and clean."

"Nah. It's Cate. Everything she touches is just...to die for."

Her fork clattered to the table. Everyone looked at her, clearly expecting her to make a perky comment. In a blink, she realized that's how this was going to have to be. Her making smart remarks, taking care not to look at Harm, keeping up a sassy conversation with them all. Acting like normal, because if she did otherwise, the thief/killer could be alerted. It's just...she wasn't used to lying.

She'd never been able to tolerate liars or lying, in fact.

"You want to know the truth," she responded to Arthur's compliment, "I didn't think this particular meal was up to par. If you guys'll bring me more fresh salmon, I promise I'll give you a dinner you'll never forget."

"Aw, Cate. You mean we'll have to fish again?" Purdue gave a mock groan, and the rest laughed. They'd had a good time fishing. Or acted as if they had.

She served vanilla honey-bee ice cream, heaped with sharp sprinkles of dark chocolate and butterscotch, but by then, she couldn't eat a thing herself. When she put the dish down for Harm, she almost put a hand on his shoulder—just wanting the connection, needing a connection. But she pulled back in time, disappeared into the galley where she could be by herself. Safe from doing the wrong thing or saying the wrong thing.

Safe from being herself.

Harm stuck tight with his men after dinner, so once Cate shined up the galley, she disappeared downstairs to her cabin, e-mailed her sisters, rinsed out some things, took a shower. She'd turn in early, she decided.

That worked like trying to make meringue with old eggs.

She got up at midnight, grumpily scooped up blankets and a tarp, and tiptoed down the aisle, then up deck. Nothing stirred. The water *slop-slurped* against the boat, and outside was colder than a well digger's ankle—but the sky was putting on a breathtaking color show, shooting silvers and purples and jeweled colors in flashes of smoke. She was diverted momentarily, watching, until she heard a sound in the pilothouse.

She whirled around—but the pilothouse was dark, locked up for the night, a pale glow of instruments reflecting on the walls but nothing else visible. She was just spooked, which was the whole reason she couldn't sleep to begin with. Toting her gear, shivering hard now, she climbed the last set of steps to the top deck.

There was no Harm here tonight—or anyone else. She told herself she was crazy to feel safer out in the open than locked in her cabin, but it wasn't that simple. There were too many men between her and an exit. And when it came down to it, the only one who'd have any reason to think she'd be way up here was Harm.

She settled down, and maybe it was the stress, but she curled up tight and felt herself dropping off to sleep almost right away.

She never heard a footstep on the stair, never heard a breath of sound. Never felt anything or sensed anything until she suddenly felt a big, heavy push. Next thing she knew, her eyes flew open and she was hurtling over the side.

Blankets were too tangled around her to get her arms free, to grab for something, anything. Something hard cracked the back of her skull...then her hip thunked, ringing hard...and then everything went black.

Harm didn't know what he'd heard, but he hadn't been sleeping...and whatever that *thunk-thud* was, the sound was discordant in the still night. His eyes popped open. He waited, but there was no other sound.

Still. It was wrong—particularly right now, when any discordant sound made him worry about another catastrophe—so he climbed from the bunk and yanked on sweats and deck shoes. Silently, he opened the cabin door and waited for several beats, trying to smell or see or sense anything that was out of the ordinary.

There was nothing. Telling himself he was being an idiot for being so hyper, he trudged upstairs, grumbled through the main salon, then the dining room, then poked in Cate's galley. Nothing wrong anywhere— except in his head.

He circled outside, stepped up to the pilothouse, checked the door—it was locked, naturally, the instrument panel lit up as it should be. Nothing unusual, nothing out of place. Since he'd come this far, he circled the foredeck, thinking maybe Cate had chosen to sleep topside again…but near the ladder, he suddenly saw the rumpled shadow on the deck.

He caught a single glimpse of blond hair tilted over the side, under the rail, and hurtled into a sprint. He skidded, almost fell—damn deck was slick—crashed on a knee as he got to her.

"Cate. Cate." She'd been sleeping top deck, just as he'd guessed, which was easy to assess from the mound of blankets and covers—and which, thank God, cushioned her fall. Still, her white face and closed eyes scared the starch out of him. He wasn't sure if or where she might be broken, but he had to shift her to a less precarious position. As swiftly as he could secure her in a safer spot on the deck, he felt the pulse at her throat.

Her heartbeat barely registered, but then suddenly beat like a drum against his fingers…at the same time her eyes opened. "Hey," she murmured, a lover's word the way she said it…only then she winced. "Ouch. What the—?"

"Shhh. Shhh. Don't move at all until we figure out what's going on. Just tell me where you hurt."

Her eyes closed for a second, scaring him halfway to death and back again, but then she came through with a list of specific damages. "Head. Hip. Pride."

He wanted to smile at the "pride," but he couldn't. Carefully, tenderly, he ran his fingers through the scarecrow-blond curls, found a spot that felt warm and damp, with a good-size lump underneath it. "I'm not sure if it's a good idea to move you."

"Don't worry about it. You're not moving me. I'm moving myself. For darn sure, I'm not staying here. *Damn*." She tried to push to a sitting position, and immediately fell back dizzily.

"You think you were born stubborn as a goat, or was it an acquired character trait? I'm serious about your not moving yet. You could have a concussion, Cate."

"Then I'll have a concussion inside, where it's nice and warm. Besides, my head's too hard to have a concussion. Trust me. Harm—"

"What?"

"Did you see who pushed me?"

He frowned. "You fell."

"I didn't fall. I was pushed—yikes!"

She was so tangled in blankets that she almost fell again…but this time fell against him. He was still reeling from the idea of someone deliberately pushing her when she crashed against him with an *oomph* and another cry of pain.

And that was it. No question she was gonna hate it—but he took charge.

Chapter 7

Cate couldn't have passed out because she wasn't some fluttery wimp who went around fainting. But when she opened her eyes, she seemed to be in Harm's stateroom, flat on his bed, with his blankets snuggled to her neck. Harm was leaning over her with a warm washcloth.

"Did I take a little nap?" she asked bewilderedly.

"Let's put it this way. If you hadn't conked out, I'd have had to hit you over the head with a frying pan. My God, you're trouble."

"I think something like a frying pan *did* hit me on the head. Holy kamoly, do I ever have a headache…." She tried to sit up and failed.

"I'm almost done. The wound's clean. I'm going to put on some antibiotic first-aid cream and cover it up, and then we'll put ice on it. Then we'll check out the rest of you."

"Hmm. I haven't played doctor since I was somewhere around five or six."

"I never gave it up. It was always one of my favorite games. Especially with girls."

"I never played it with girls."

"That's why you probably gave it up. Playing with girls is fun."

"Why in God's name are we joking around?"

"Because," he said, "I almost had a heart attack when I saw you on the deck. And I'm trying to get past that so I can start thinking straight."

"Let's not rush into thinking," she agreed. Consciousness was coming back. Enough to be aware of Harm's bare chest. He'd gotten blood on his shirt. Her blood. She could see the stain on his shirt from the top of the bureau. More relevant, she could see the patches of blond hair on his chest, the cords of muscle in his upper arms, the intensely passionate fury in his eyes. You didn't hurt people Harm cared about, she mused. He just wasn't the kind of man you'd want to rile. "Your bed is significantly more comfortable than mine."

"I'm glad you like it, since you'll be bunking in here from now on."

"I'm pretty positive my boss isn't going to like that."

Harm pleasantly suggested what Ivan could do to himself if the captain raised any objection whatsoever. After that, he leaned over her, so close she could breathe in the scent of his warm, warm skin. Unfortunately, his only intent was to put a bandage on the back of her head—a project that had as much chance of succeeding as a frost in the Amazon.

"Harm. It won't stick. Besides which, I want to wash my hair."

"Of course it'll stick. It has to stick. How else am I going to put ice on it? Obviously, I can't put ice on the direct sore." He motioned to where he'd clearly fetched a bowl of ice from the galley. She wondered how the Sam Hill long she had been knocked out.

"You could put a couple cubes in a plastic bag. Then put the washcloth between my skin and the bag."

He looked annoyed—probably because she used the same patient tone she'd use with a small child. But he did it. "I guess that'll do, Ms. MacGyver. So on to the next problem. Your hip. It sounds as if it was one of your crash connection points."

"Afraid so. I'm just thankful I was so covered up in sleeping bags and blankets that the fall was cushioned. Still, I have to admit it hurts like hell."

"Cate." His tone turned gentle, serious. "I want to see it. No funny business, no joking. I'd just feel better if we both saw how bad it is. I also think we should make sure there are no other breaks or injuries that need attention."

She looked at him. "You know…I've been thinking about being naked with you."

"Have you?"

"But not in this context."

"I think we should put it in that other context as soon as possible. But right now, I'm worried you're a lot more hurt than you're letting on. When you fall that distance, you're talking a major clunk, Cookie."

"Don't call me Cookie. And believe me, I'd be baying at the top of my lungs if I had anything serious to complain about. I'm an A-grade whiner."

"No, you aren't and no, you wouldn't," Harm said patiently. "You're tough as nails. Strong as a rock. And stubborn as a hound."

"Didn't your mother teach you any better than this? If you want to seduce a woman, you need to use sweet talk, not insults." She was looking right at him, and he was looking right back, but Cate felt what he was doing. Peeling off the blanket. Finding the drawstring of her sleeping pants. And then she felt his big, bare hand on her flesh. She slapped her own hand over his to stop him.

"My mom tried to teach me manners. You'd love her. She kept this little switch on the top of the refrigerator, something on par with a tree twig. Threatened me with beatings my whole childhood, but never once laid a finger on me."

"She should have," Cate said darkly. With infinite gentleness, he'd lifted her hand. With even more infinite gentleness, that intrusive, intimate hand slowly stroked down her body, from the sides of her breasts to her ribs to the start of her bony hip and around. His touch, his tenderness, was the lovemaking of a fantasy—the big, strong guy able to melt for and with the right woman.

Only this wasn't lovemaking, and there was no fantasy. The glaring overhead light blinded her and made her feel overvulnerable.

Damn it. She hated feeling vulnerable. Even with a lover, she picked the time, the place, the circumstance. She chose what happened and how.

"You can tell my mom that she should have smacked me when I was a kid. She'll totally agree with you. I can remember having an argument with her when I was in high school—something about using the car. Anyway, she got on a footstool so she'd be tall enough to shake her finger in my face. Beats me why. She won every argument we ever had anyway—*damn it,* Cate."

His soothing tone and gentle tenderness abruptly disappeared. He didn't yank or tear, but once he discovered the mighty bruise on her hip, he forgot that she might have some serious modesty issues. It wasn't as if the location of the injury was any surprise to her. She already figured it was going to be the mother of all bruises.

From the way Harm was swearing, it was already the mother of all bruises times ten. And unfortunately, once he'd discovered that lumpy bruise, he turned dead serious about checking every inch of the rest of her right then, in detail, fast, no arguing with him. "This hurt?"

"Of course it hurts. You're poking my shoulder."

"Shut up, Cate. Answer the question. How about here?"

It was that "shut up" that made the tears well. She squeezed her eyes closed so the stupid things wouldn't fall. It was downright silly to get all buttery over a "shut up" when no woman in the universe would think of it as a love word. But it was. With him, it was. She saw it in his eyes, heard it in the gravel-roughness in his voice, felt it in the rage in his careful, careful hands.

"Okay. The spot behind the shoulder. And the hip. And my head. But nothing's broken—I can tell and you can tell. So I think you should cover me up with some warm blankets and bring me some wine and be nice."

"I think I should find who did this to you and..." His breath caught. "It's my fault this happened to you, Cate."

"It certainly is. You should have been up on the top deck, waiting for the bad guy to show up and stop him from pushing me off. Talk about dereliction of responsibility. You're a cad through and through."

"I'm going to the galley for more ice. Lots and lots of ice. And more bags or something to put it in. You're getting ice on the hip as well as on your head. We're getting that swelling down. And you're getting woken up every couple hours just to be sure of the concussion business. Now. Try giving me a hard time."

She considered it. He was obviously enjoying turning into Mr.-Own-The-Universe-Bossy. But for a couple of minutes, she was increasingly feeling like a battered kickball. A little silence and rest might help her get a better grip.

But Harm seemed to return to the cabin in three seconds flat, carrying heaping bags of ice and a dark scowl. "It's got to hurt darned bad if it's making you cry."

"I wasn't crying! Sheesh!" She watched him turn down the lights, flick on the one in the master head, dimming the room. If the damned man was going to be considerate enough to let her hide her expression in the darkness, he really was going to make her cry. The ugly, loud kind of crying. "Harm—"

"Yeah?" He'd covered the makeshift ice bags in towels, eased the one between the headboard and the goose egg on her head, then cushioned one against the monster bruise on her thigh. Then started covering and tucking.

"I think Yale overheard me telling the captain about the peppermint."

If he added any more blankets, she was going to roast. But he looked at her so sharply, she changed her mind about complaining.

"You think so, hmm?" Finally, he pushed off his shoes and eased down on the mattress next to her, barely taking any covers, careful not to jolt her in any way. "My first reaction to that is to go kill Yale, Cookie. But on second thought…he could have passed that information on to the other two. So there's no guarantee he was the pusher, only that he was probably the catalyst to your getting hurt. If he did pass on your death-by-peppermint theory to the others, I'd think you'd be prey to some teasing tomorrow. That is, if any of them are brash enough—or smart enough—to bring it up openly."

He'd spooned around her so protectively that, hurts or no hurts, she started to feel snuggly and safe. And turned on—which struck her as a completely lunatic response, considering how beat-up she was. "Harm?"

"Okay. You get to say one more thing. But then you're closing your eyes and getting some rest."

"I was just thinking that tomorrow morning, I should

tell everyone at breakfast how I fell asleep top deck, fell off, and got really bruised. Make a point of saying how stupid and careless I was. Not imply in any way that I believe someone deliberately pushed me."

He thought. "That's a great idea, Cate. It's much safer if no one thinks we're on to them. In fact, I can bring up your death-by-peppermint theory and make out like I think it's funny—for the same reason—to make the culprit think he's safe. However…"

"However what?"

"However, you won't be making breakfast tomorrow, Toots. You're going to be in here. Safe and sound."

"You call me Toots or Cookie again, Harm, and that's it. I won't sleep with you, no matter how much you beg me."

He scooched down, just another notch, pressed the softest whisper of a kiss on her brow. "Aw, yeah, you will." And then, "What a fabulous little body you've got. Perfect. Curved in all the right places. Strong and sweet."

"Yeah. I know," she said, and damn the man, but he forced her to fall asleep on a smile.

She slept, but Harm couldn't. First off, he couldn't rest because he had to check on her every few minutes—to make sure she was covered, to make sure the ice packs were still cold and not leaking. And obviously, to make sure she wasn't hurting.

And since he was stuck not sleeping, he kept turning over the last two days of events in his mind. It seemed petrifyingly likely that someone had tried to kill Cate—probably the same someone who'd killed Fiske, who was the same someone at the source of the formula disappearance.

That was easy enough to conclude. But it didn't help him any more than it had before to identify the culprit.

He woke Cate every two hours to check her pupils, kiss her brow and order her back to sleep. By 5:00 a.m., though, he gave up trying to sleep himself. The only thing he'd gotten from the long, endless night so far was an evocative long, endless hard-on from sleeping next to her.

The pervasiveness of that hard-on made him aggravatingly aware that he was becoming more attached to that woman than a thorn on a rose. He barely knew her, yet here he was losing sleep, feeling responsible, feeling a sense of connection and pull and hunger to be around her.

Groggy-eyed, he headed up on deck and went straight for the elegant, old-fashioned coffee urn. It looked awful to him, but when push came to shove, it was just a machine. He'd made coffee in tougher spots in the army, so he wasn't worried he couldn't figure it out.

He prowled around Cate's galley for coffee beans, something to measure water, then paced around, waiting for the others to wake up. The sky was blurry, a mix of doughy clouds and murky light, and didn't discernibly change over the next hour. By then he'd worn holes in the deck, pacing around and realizing—not for the first time—that he was really good at doing, and really bad at having to wait and not act.

Finally, though, Ivan emerged from the crew quarters. Harm didn't leap on him like a rabid dog, but the captain had barely gotten out a yawn before he barked, "Is it okay with you if I get into the pilothouse? Use the radio?"

"Sure." Ivan filled a mug, carted it with him outside to unlock and step into the pilothouse. The captain hadn't shaved, had sucked down his share of whiskey the night before and had the swollen eyes to prove it. Still, he was no one's fool. He set him up with the radio, then plopped in the captain chair, out of the way. "What happened?"

"Cate was hurt last night."

Ivan's eyes sharpened. "How, when, where and what?"

Harm talked; Ivan started up the engines, and both of them took turns at the radio, communicating to the mainland and Baranof Springs. By then, Arthur showed up, holding a mug, saying, "Who in God's name made this sludge? Where's Cate? What's going on?"

His three guys all looked as if they'd had a rough night, but none had a guilt sign tattooed on their foreheads, nothing to give away any more information than Harm already had. The story he told them—while serving a bunch of fruit in a bowl and army oatmeal—was that Cate had fallen the night before. She'd apparently headed topside to do some stargazing, dozed off and then fell.

The men all expressed concern that sounded sincere. Purdue eventually tried to lighten the atmosphere by lifting his cereal spoon, trying to make a joke. "I've never had much religion, but I'm willing to fall to my knees and pray that she's feeling good enough to make the next meal. Are you sure this is oatmeal and not cement?"

Arthur was in no mood for humor. "Harm, I think we should cancel this trip completely and go home. There's just too much going wrong. It's as if we're jinxed."

Yale immediately backed up Arthur. "It doesn't matter what the authorities said. They can't keep us here. If they have any more questions about Fiske, they can call us or something. No one can stop us from going home."

"It's not that simple," Harm said.

"Sure, it is."

Harm said, "There isn't a doctor, but there is a PA in Baranof Springs, and we can be there in just a couple more hours. The lump on Cate's head is one big slugger. I really believe a medical person should check her out before going anywhere else." He exchanged glances with Ivan. Both also knew, from the radio transmissions earlier, that the Juneau pathologist had returned from his fishing trip, and they could possibly hear more about Fiske's autopsy later that day or tomorrow. Harm's priority was Cate. But he was wary of making any sudden moves without all the information he could gather first.

"So we stay through today," Arthur agreed, but his tone still reflected tension. "I just think we should head home right after that. I'm really uneasy with all this. We still don't even know what happened to Fiske."

"I know what Cate thought happened," Purdue piped in. "Yale told me he heard her talking to the captain.

Said she went to make more peppermint cookies for us and found all her peppermint oil—or extract, or whatever it is—gone. She was worried Fiske got into it. Might have gotten sick from it somehow."

So Yale *had* overheard that conversation, Harm mused. Just as Cate thought. But if both Purdue and Yale knew about Cate's theory, neither still had a motivation to push her off the top deck—at least none Harm could think of.

Arthur edged back his chair. "Actually, using peppermint on a toothache is an old-fashioned remedy. Maybe that was what Fiske was doing in the galley. We all know how he was addicted to sweets. Maybe a tooth started going bad on him."

Harm finished the oatmeal and had another coffee. Neither tasted that bad to him. Of course, he wasn't concentrating on food. He was studying his men, and suffering enough frustration to claw walls. None of them showed any sign of guilt. There were no hidden looks, no apparent nerves. The whole mood of the guys was darker than gloom, though, until Cate suddenly showed up in the doorway.

She looked like something the cat dragged in out of the rain. Her hair, never styled at the best of times, stuck up in ragamuffin spikes around a blue-scarf bandage. She'd pulled on big, droopy sweats over big, droopy socks, and could barely traverse the room without limping. Panic buzzed his heartbeat. "What the Sam Hill are you doing up here?" he demanded.

She shot him a look reserved usually for puppies who'd piddled. "Well, I'll be. Did you suddenly turn into my boss?" She shot a scandalized look at the table's contents. "Are you boys trying to eat this? And who burned the coffee? I could smell it all the way below deck."

"Cate—" He thought she'd agreed to stay in his cabin, locked up tight, where she'd be safe.

"I was just en route to the head when some of the conversation filtered downstairs. I thought I heard that y'all were going to postpone going home because of me. That's silly. I'm fine." She limped over to the coffee urn. "I don't need a doctor. You guys should do whatever it is you want or need to do. I admit, I may not be up to much cooking today…but honest to Pete, even if I were bedridden in a body cast, I can keep you guys fed better than this."

Harm was about to get testy about all the slurs to his breakfast making, but abruptly he realized what she was doing. The men immediately took *his* side, bullying her into the necessity of having someone medical check her out in Baranof Springs. Even if they all wanted to go home, it wasn't as if a few hours' difference was going to matter.

She poured a mug of his "burned" coffee and made it all the way around the table to the seat next to him. She never winced, never outwardly showed how much she was hurting. But she still eased down next to him like a kitten next to her lion. He realized abruptly that the damn woman was making all this effort for his sake—playing his team, her way, to help him get what he wanted, which was more time here in Alaska.

Actually, what he wanted was to scoop her onto his

lap and hold her indefinitely. He wanted to soothe those bruises away, make her feel safe and warm, yell at her for being such a numbskull for climbing the stairs.

He could hardly do any of those things—particularly when she took another sip from her mug, and spouted further gross, effusive insults about his inability to make coffee.

"We could kill rats with this, I guess. But…I don't think we have any. Possibly we could clean all the sinks? I'm pretty sure this swill would kill even the most optimistic germ nature ever created—"

"Sheesh. You think that's enough ribbing?" Harm played up that his feelings were hurt. Maybe they even were, a little.

"I don't know, guys. You think that's enough ribbing?"

Of course the guys didn't think it was enough ribbing. They'd never teased him before. Cate was egging them on. And in the meantime, Hans was edging into the dock at Baranof Springs. At which time, Ivan announced orders to all passengers to bring a towel and their bathing suits.

"Right," was the standard incredulous response.

Ivan said, "I mean it. Follow the road through town, up the hill. On the right side of the waterfalls—which are colder than a witch's tit in a brass bra, pardon my French, Cate—are hot springs. All bigger than hot tubs. Think we'd all benefit from an hour's soak. And that sure includes Cate."

"Sounds great," Cate said.

She looked him straight in the eye when she said

it. Harm let out an internal sigh of relief. At least one thing was going right. She'd get off at the Springs, get the medic to check her out, and at least he could know she was physically all right before dealing with the next crisis.

Cate barely made it back below deck before collapsing on her bunk. For the first time, the cabin didn't strike her as claustrophobic. She just plain didn't care. Her head hurt. Her hip hurt. She felt whipped and battered and weak as a baby bird.

It was intolerable. But she was pretty sure she'd put on a good show for the guys—especially for Harm—and if they'd all just get off the damned boat, she could get some rest and peace. Yes, of course, she expected they'd notice she didn't join the shore group...but she also suspected none of them particularly wanted to infringe on her female bastion/boudoir.

She should have known that wouldn't work for Harm. Heaven knew how much time had passed before she heard his knuckles rapping on her cabin door.

"I'm sleeping," she called out.

"You're going to get checked out."

"All I need is rest. Go on with the group."

"I could tear down the door, but that seems awkward. It looks to be made of steel. That won't stop me, but I'm afraid it'll make a lot of damage—"

She hurtled off the bunk, across the cabin, and yanked open the door with one hand on her head. "Go away."

"You are such a faker. Making everybody believe you're just fine, just a little bruised. Did you think you were going to fool me, too?" He entered the cabin, which meant there wasn't enough oxygen for one, much less for two people trying to move around. She sank back on the bunk, since Mr. Busybody seemed determined to paw around, locate her jacket and shoes. "You're not only seeing this medic, but if I don't like the medic, I'm getting a plane in here and getting you to a hospital on the mainland."

"You and what army?"

"I don't need an army."

She opened her mouth to give him what for—and it was a what for that was going to include a blistering set down—when his tone softened to rough gravel.

"Cate, if you need me to carry you, I can and will."

Damn him. It was that tone that made her want to melt. And she wasn't the melting type. "I really want to just sleep. And this is a great chance for you to be alone with the men. Push their limits. Dig until you find out stuff."

"Yup, it would be. But there's a time to worry about murder and larceny. And a time when a guy needs to take care of his girl. It's a no-brainer which counts more."

He didn't actually carry her. She climbed to the main deck, walked strong as an ox off the boarding ramp. The air was brisk, eagles perched on high spruce boughs, watching the fish in the harbor. A dozen other yachts and fishing boats were docked close by. The yachts looked as if they cost millions and millions. The fishing boats looked as if they'd survived two world wars and then some. A slope of land showed a scattering of buildings stretched on what was clearly the only road. And a silver-diamond waterfall bounded down a rock crevice. All of it took her attention…at least until she caved.

Harm caught her before she fell, swooped her up in his arms as if she were a damned baby. And she held on, head snugged against his neck, as if she'd have fallen if she hadn't.

"I'm not your girl," she said.

"No?"

"We haven't even slept together."

"Yeah, we did."

"We haven't made love. That kind of sleeping."

"That isn't sleeping. Trust me, if you didn't know that before, you will after I get through with you."

"Harm. Get serious." She couldn't seem to keep her eyes open, but that didn't mean she wasn't fully serious. "We're not a pair. Can't possibly be. You're a conservative guy. You need a wife who's into a house in the suburbs, commitment, an intrepid Volvo for the kids, responsibility. I could live out of a carpet bag and have space left over. I don't have a clue how to be a wife. I don't even like money. I wouldn't work for you. Trust me."

"I probably wouldn't work for you, either. I've had two divorces. Don't be forgetting that."

She frowned, confused. "I haven't forgotten that. But like I told you, it's irrelevant. I don't doubt you married women who couldn't handle you. You're a complete pain."

"So that's settled," he said, with such a tone of satisfaction that she was confused.

"What's settled?"

"That you're my girl. And that we seem to be at the, um, clinic now."

Clinic? When Cate turned her head, she saw a cedar door open, and a small boy emerge with his dog. The kid was a scrapper, skinny, ragged cap, but healthy-looking. The dog looked like a sled dog, beautiful and elegant and soft-eyed, with a giant white bandage on his left paw.

"You're taking me to a vet?" she asked disbelievingly.

Harm didn't look any happier. "Beats me. Captain said it was the third building, go upstairs to the second floor. That's where we are."

The place seemed to be an apartment, not a clinic, where a big bear of a man lumbered through a living room to greet them. Toys littered the floor. A toddler was pulling a noisy push toy. The big bearded guy scooped up the squirt and bellowed for his wife, who showed up in the doorway, wiping her hands on a dish towel.

"So you're the one who had the fall on the boat?" she said. "Come on in. Let's have a look."

The laundry room had a stretcher, which apparently doubled as an exam table. Harm came in with her—not that she asked him—but he clearly didn't think much of the setup. She did. Cate could see intelligence and common sense in the woman's eyes, her whole no-nonsense demeanor. "We usually have a doctor around here, retired from Anchorage, but in the summer, he's hit or miss, off on a fishing trip anytime he can find someone to go with him."

"I hear there's a lot of that going around," Cate said.

The woman chuckled. "Anyway, I'm what's left over. Used to be a surgical nurse on the mainland, picked up credentials as a P.A. No fancy degrees, nothing extra, but I know enough to get you flown out of here if we think there's a reason."

"I just took a fall," Cate said. "I'm fine. Just going to be bruised up and sore for a little while."

"It was a serious fall," Harm interjected. "From one deck down to the next."

"But I was asleep. And covered with blankets, really cushioned."

"Aha. You two are doing a lot of talking. How about if I do a lot of looking?" Ten minutes later, she said, "You took a good fall and you're going to be bruised and sore for a little while."

"See? What'd I tell you?" Cate said immediately to Harm once they were outside. "So I'm going to those hot springs. Sounds like a good place to soak. And the lady the same as said I'm totally okay."

"What the lady didn't realize was that you've got a head harder than rock and can't be trusted to show good judgment." But Harm was back to ribbing her. His whole mood eased after she'd been given a decent bill of health. He hooked an arm around her shoulder as they strolled up the street toward the waterfall and springs.

"So now we can concentrate on murder and madness," she said with satisfaction.

"Now *I* can concentrate on murder and madness."

Cate didn't argue. Right then, although she'd never

admit it aloud, she felt too darned weak to walk all the way back to the boat. She figured the short trek to the springs was all she could handle.

That didn't mean she wasn't going to help him, though.

He didn't have a choice in the matter.

Chapter 8

Harm climbed on the rock behind Cate and stopped dead still. The harbor and town were nice enough, but no one would guess the view beyond the slope and into the trees.

The trek wasn't long from the P.A.'s place. The splash of a silver waterfall was always in sight, tumbling over rocks and glistening off pines, but the sudden path leading to the shaded glen was like a step into a mystic paradise. Pools carpeted the rocky landscape, a half dozen or more. Warm, fragrant steam rose from each one. Ferns and pines caught the occasional ribbon of sunlight from above. Spears of light reflected on dripping ferns and moss, the magic interrupted only— only—by the raucous sound of men's laughter.

A few other people were wandering around, but Ivan, Hans, Yale, Purdue and Arthur had staked out one sizable pool next to the waterfall. They whistled and hooted hellos the instant the newcomers were spotted. Cate, in spite of the bandage on her head, started laughing. "Well, if this isn't a skinny-dipping paradise."

Harm scowled. It was. The captain had advised the guys to bring bathing suits and towels, but that didn't mean they had—and the drifts of steam floating above the water was hardly concealing. Worse yet, Cate pushed off her shoes and started tugging off her jacket.

"Wait a minute," he said with alarm.

She shot him a grin. "Afraid I'm naked under this, handsome?"

That's exactly what he was afraid of. She hadn't done much yet to convince him that she wasn't fearless to the point of foolhardy—not to mention that he didn't want anyone seeing her naked but him.

A path of slippery, wet rocks led to the pool. Harm was never less than a step behind Cate, stripping as fast as she was, hustling to keep up with her. As she shimmied out of her pants, he saw with relief that she wore exercise shorts and a T-shirt. It was a long way from the neck-to-toe covering he wished she were wearing, but at least the essentials were shielded. And the guys, of course, were looking.

Before he could stop her—not that he could have—she'd edged over the rocks and into the pool. "Harm..." She reached back for his hand, which just happened to be right where she could reach it. He steadied her as she sank in, right up to her neck. She released a long, blissful sigh.

"Wow. This feels like total heaven and then some… especially on some of these bruises. I'm never leaving. Maybe someone can bring us food and drink up here."

The guys started a steady round of joking, but the serenity of the place eventually quieted everyone. The ceiling of green pines, the warm springs, the impossibly fresh air seemed to melt everyone's stress. Even Harm unwillingly started to relax. Cate's nearness could have worn down a stone. Her knee kept brushing his, her shoulder, as if she were deliberately staying in touch with him, communicating underwater something private and real….

At least until she suddenly piped up with a question for the group. "Hey, you guys, while we're all together, I want to hear some more about this cancer drug you all created."

He figured he'd misheard her. Someone had pushed her from the top deck last night. She couldn't possibly be thinking about baiting a bear.

"Seems crazy to talk about work on a gorgeous day like this," Purdue said lazily.

"Especially when we've got a half-naked goddess among us," Yale concurred.

Harm leveled his youngest employee with a razor-sharp stare, but Cate only chuckled. She leaned back, closed her eyes. "You're right about the goddess, guys. But I lost my family so young. Maybe it wasn't from cancer, but I relate to how awful it is to lose loved ones. How helpless you feel when you can't do anything about it. Even how angry. And yet your team picked a couple of the toughest cancers…."

"That was Dougal's doing. Harm's uncle," Arthur shared. "He lost his wife to cancer. That was his motivation."

"And for the rest of us," Purdue said, "it wouldn't have been any fun to pick the easy cancers to work with."

"There are easy cancers?"

"Not easy." Yale was starting to rev up now. It was always hard for him to resist talking about his favorite subject. "Most people don't have a reason to understand cancer—that it isn't one illness or one thing. It's a whole class of diseases. The only thing they have in common is that a bunch of cells suddenly grow out of control. The key answer is always why. We know environment and heredity are primary factors, but there's more to it."

Purdue picked up the thread. "Basically, there are four main kinds. Carcinomas are malignant tumors that grow from a base of epithelial cells. They're the most common. They're like—breast, prostate, lung, colon. Then there are sarcomas. Those are malignant tumors that grow from connective tissue."

"Then there's lymphoma and leukemia," Yale interjected. "Essentially, those emanate from blood-forming cells. And then there are germ-cell tumors. Those come from totipotent cells…."

"Okay, okay. Overloading," Cate said. "You're getting too complicated for me. Just go back to one of the cancers you're working on. Like pancreatic. What makes that one different?"

Even Arthur got into it now. "For one thing, it's one

of the toughest to cure. It's also one of the worst killers. It's just plain ugly."

Cate nodded. "Now, you're talking language I can understand. But what makes that cancer so hard to cure?"

"Three things," Purdue said. "All about the cells. They're tiny and they grow like weeds and they hide. Actually, it's the hiding factor that's always been the worst problem."

"But you guys found an answer for that?"

"Exactly." Yale leaned his head back. "It's complicated. But to put it in basic terms, what we discovered was a chemical that turned on those sucker-small cells. They grow neon bright when exposed, even through dense tissue."

Harm held his breath. None of them talked this way to outsiders, primarily because of security and privacy. And they shouldn't. But Cate was somehow able to charm money from a beggar…and he hungered for the chance to hear how each of the men responded.

"So how'd you all find this formula where nobody else could?" Cate asked.

"Initially, it was Dougal's breakthrough—Harm's uncle. He didn't have the formula pinned down, but he established the breakthrough idea. Then when he got ill, Purdue took over some of the lab work. Then me. Took a while before we were getting consistent results. Then we started the real trials."

"Which was…when?"

"Over the last two years. The compound passed every damn test we could put it through. We have it. We *had* it." Purdue's voice carried the whine of frustration. "The next step was final FDA approval, but there was no reason that would have been denied. We had all the legal grounds set up. It was ours. The company's. We all had a stake in it. There was just a waiting period until the final stuff came through. There was no doubt in any of our minds that we had the real thing."

Arthur said, "I'm roasting here. Think I'm getting out, wandering back toward the ship."

The comment came out of the blue, stopped the discussion cold—and started an exodus. Simultaneously, the guys started to move, standing up, groaning when their flesh suddenly contacted cool-cold fresh air. Instead of joining the others, Cate leaned her head back and closed her eyes.

Harm wasn't about to budge without her. Immediately, though, he noticed that her perky questions and zesty smiles all faded once the men disappeared from sight. The clear water revealed her lithe, slim body. She wasn't soft. Her calves were tight, molded from walking and exercise, her hips more bone than padding. A few sunbeams sneaked through the green canopy overhead, lighting on freckles and a skinny nose, on bare lips.

She looked nothing like any woman he'd ever loved.

But he looked at her, and wondered if he'd ever loved before.

"You wade right into trouble, don't you?" he murmured.

"Yup. It was one of the things my foster mom taught me. Never avoid trouble if you can help it. It's the old shark-in-the-water thing. If you don't turn around and face it, you have no way of knowing if trouble's on your tail."

"Are you going to be able to make it back to the boat?"

"Maybe. In a bit." She opened one eye. One sharp blue eye. "I'm not sick, Harm."

"I know."

"It just hurts. The bruise on the hip more than the head. But really, the rest of me is okay."

"The rest of you is more than okay," he corrected her.

There now. He got a smile. Softer than butter. Lustrous. But then it disappeared. "There's a huge piece missing, Harm. Didn't you hear it?"

"What do you mean?"

"Your guys. Your problem. There's this huge hole that doesn't make sense. Everybody's got a loyalty to this formula you all developed. Everybody values the team, what they were doing. Everybody could see success coming, personal and financial. There doesn't seem to be a single visible gain for anyone to steal the formula, when everyone was already going to get rich, already going to get tons of lauds and credit. So what could possibly motivate the man to steal it?"

Harm was beginning to have his suspicions. But he still told Cate the frustrating truth. "I don't know."

"There has to be something we're missing."

"Yes."

"It's driving me nuts. Trying to figure it out." She opened both her eyes then. "Maybe...Fiske died of natural causes. Maybe my fall was somehow accidental. Maybe things only look dire and dangerous and they really aren't." She frowned. "Harm, I totally realize this isn't really my business or my problem. But I'm at least a fresh pair of eyes. And I didn't know anyone before, so I can be objective. So I'm not trying to bug you, I really hoped I could bring something to your table, seriously help. Except…"

"Except that your mind's spinning sideways?"

"Oh, man. You said it."

"So how about if we see…if we can make your mind spin in a whole different way? A good way," he promised. He valued everything she'd said, but it was too much. The more she hurtled into his problems, the deeper he hurtled into her character. He liked that foolhardy character of hers, but for a while, he wanted her to quit worrying. He wanted her to quit hurting.

He wanted to figure out how deep he was in with her.

He found out.

Damn fast, he found out.

Careful of her sore hip, even more careful of the lump on her head, he scooped her closer, using his arms as a cushion for her neck. And then he kissed her. Not softly. Not carefully. But with everything he had.

He took her mouth. Her tongue. Her breath.

A few other people had been enjoying the springs, but no one was in sight now. The only sounds were the splashing waterfalls, the whisper of leaves, the shallow intake of her breath, the beat of her heart…and his.

Somewhere, in the rush of water, the heat, the thick

scent of pine, she turned liquid for him. Her limbs flowed over his, around his. Her lips turned slippery-soft, under his, with his.

An hour before, he thought she didn't have enough clothes on. Now he realized she had way, way too many. Thankfully, they were soaked snug to her skin. It wasn't as good as naked, but he could still feel her. Her bones, her small, lithe muscles, the cushion of breast and tummy.

She murmured…something in the language of music. A call, a whisper, a tune of longing.

Desire barreled through his pulse like a racehorse at the gate. He stroked the length of her tenderly, with precious care for where she could be sore or bruised… Yet still, he found nipple, found treasure beneath the waistband of her pants, hair that curled around his fingers, inviting him into her private nest.

She murmured again. This time the sound she made was more of a feline hiss. She stroked him too, but not with tenderness or care. Her fingers made prints, denting his back and shoulders, down his sides. Her hands, her mouth, enticed him to forget where they were, who they were, and when she suddenly twisted her full weight on top of him, he went down.

He surfaced almost immediately, sputtering, almost laughing…until he saw the reckless intent in her eyes. It was her turn to slide a hand down his torso, to dip into damp pants, to find the hot, hard core of him and squeeze. It wasn't a nice squeeze. It wasn't a sweet, shy squeeze. It was an I'm-gonna-have-you kind of squeeze.

"Cate. Think. You're too sore," he hissed.

"Oh, well," she murmured.

"We're in public."

"I'm afraid that's your problem. I told you not to start something the next time you didn't intend to finish." She was teasing. Until she wasn't. Her hands suddenly framed his face. "Harm. I don't know where we're going. But I know darn well we're moving."

"You think you can count on me to say no?"

"I think I can count on you to come through for me. And I'm not sure if you know it. But you can trust me."

That was the thing. Just the thing. He didn't trust anyone, hadn't in years, couldn't remember if he ever had. Yet there was something in her, something different. And for the first time since hell froze over, he felt an unwilling yielding…a wanting to believe, a need to believe in trust again.

She spurred him all the more, because he knew she trusted no one, either.

It was exquisitely clear that she'd abandoned trust when the world crashed on her head as a child, and she'd never given life a chance to hurt her like that again. But she was giving that chance to him. Opening that damned scary door.

And suddenly he was kissing her again, the talking done, nothing else in his head or heart but her. Every instinct condensed into the most basic urge and surge—to take her. Own her. To be owned right back.

The water that had seemed so luxuriously sensual now felt constrictive. He couldn't move fast in that liquid flow. Her clothes refused to easily peel off, and when he moved, they both seemed to embrace in a languid spin where she ended up under water, then he did, both of them laughing…then not.

He wanted her. Right then. Now. Yesterday. And once he plunged inside her, he wasn't letting her go. Maybe ever.

"Yes," she said, in a whisper that roared in his ears.

He was there. At the nest of her, the crest of her, in a tangle of legs and clothes and heat and fire. Ready to plunge. When he heard voices from below the hill.

"*Harm! Cate! Harm!* Hurry! Something's wrong with the captain! Where *are* you two?"

Darn hard to run when her head hurt and her side hurt and most of all, her heart hurt. Harm would have been deep inside her. Two seconds. That was all it would have taken. He was right *there*…and so was she, emotionally and physically and mentally, when she'd heard Arthur's frantic cry, then Yale and Purdue.

She'd locked eyes helplessly with Harm for all of a millisecond. Then they'd both surged from the water, gasped from the cold, grabbed clothes and started chugging down the hill. Harm kept waiting for her, trying to help her.

"Harm, don't wait for me. I'll get there. You just go see what's wrong with Ivan."

But he wouldn't leave her. You'd think she needed a babysitter. The only thing she needed right then was a heart-sitter, Cate thought, because repercussions were starting to filter into her brain about what she'd done—or what she'd been about to do. No matter how much she wanted to straighten out some things with Harm, though, there was no possible time.

Down the hill, past the scattering of buildings, halfway down the dock to the boat, Ivan was on the ground, clutching his stomach and bellowing. "I'm fine! I'm just sick! Get me on board and leave me alone!"

Hans's gentle face reflected confusion and worry. Harm hustled between the group and crouched down. "What are we dealing with?"

"Hurling. That's what we're dealing with. Disgusting, but there it is."

"Like food poisoning? Something you had here at the café? Something we could need a medic for?"

"All I need is my own bunk, my own head, some privacy. And time. I'm not the wrong kind of sick. I just want to get the hell out of Dodge."

By the time Cate reached Ivan, the captain was using increasingly colorful language…and he'd been sick over the dockside right there, which made all the men step back several feet. Except for Harm. Cate knelt down, carefully poked the captain's sides, felt his forehead for fever, checked his pulse, looked for signs of shock.

Harm didn't ask what she was doing, just echoed, "I checked for the same things, but it's been years since I had first aid in the army. What do you think?"

"I don't see any signs of anything serious, like appendicitis…."

"Would you all get away from me? If I'm gonna hurl, I don't like an audience. And I'm not going to a hospital. I'm going to my boat."

"Quit being a child, Ivan," Cate said.

He said, "You're fired."

"Yeah, yeah."

Everyone participated in getting Ivan aboard and below, which was probably why it took forever. En route, all Harm's men were singing the same tune. Enough was enough. Catastrophes were following them like ants at a picnic. It was time to call this trip off and get home.

Late afternoon, Harm left the pilothouse in search of Cate. As he might have guessed, she was in the galley. He'd barely opened the door before he was bombarded by enticing and exotic smells. Bowls and pans and utensils cluttered every counter. Cate, garbed in an apron and a T-shirt that read Incrediby Good-Looking And Built To Last was shimmying to rock and roll in her head—at least until he startled her by opening the door.

"What are you doing? You should be resting!"

"I am, I am." She motioned. "I figured on some Yukon sourdough bread pudding—because we had some day-old bread, so might as well find a good use for it. Then saffron risotto cakes. Herbed tomatoes. And then chops with a warm-belly barbecue sauce…."

He scraped a hand through his hair. "Cookie. You're hurt. You're exhausted. The captain's sick. Everything's a disaster. So maybe you still felt responsible for coming up with dinner for the group, but what would have been wrong with some peanut butter and jelly sandwiches?"

"Well…nothing. But this isn't work for me, Harm.

It's stress relief. Honest. And in the meantime, what'd you find out?" She seemed to read his expression.

"Autopsy results. What is warm-belly barbecue sauce?"

"Something that's guaranteed to put hair on your chest." She flashed him, lifted her long-sleeved T-shirt—showed him braless breasts, bitsy, adorable—then swiftly covered up again. "Which you'll find out, via taste, at dinner. In the meantime, you get nothing more until you fill me in. What'd the coroner in Juneau say?"

He wasn't going to make it through this trip. Embezzlement, theft, murder, maybe poisoning. And this woman who could spin his world on its axis in two seconds flat, without half trying. He started to answer the question, found his throat too dry to emit sound. Tried again. "I forget the formal phrase they used. But the cause of death was essentially a heart attack."

"All right."

"Like you said—his throat and esophagus were raw. Some substance had to cause it, but they couldn't pin down a chemical or poison."

"Which there wouldn't be. For peppermint. Not like it's an illegal or managed substance." She opened the gimballed oven, pulled out what looked to be a big, round pudding thing with a crust. It smelled like sin. Sin times ten. He instinctively moved toward it, but she blocked him with the royal finger. "Go on," she said.

"The bottom line is that the pathologist couldn't pin down anything that would be a court-provable homicide. I repeated the peppermint question. He acknowledged that could have created the problem—but it still doesn't prove or establish how that happened or exactly how it might have contributed to Fiske's death. His heart suffered a massive arrest."

She started splashing all kinds of unknown things into a bowl, swirling them together with a wooden spatula. "So it doesn't matter if peppermint killed him?"

"It matters. But the substance itself doesn't prove that he deliberately chose to take in the peppermint. Or to take too much of it. Or if it was forced on him. There's no bruising or verifiable evidence of force." He didn't want to talk about this. He wanted Cate back at the springs, couldn't stop replaying how close they'd come to making love. Her eyes, her mouth, her hands. The emotions bursting from her, flying off him. He couldn't explain it, what was happening with them—but it had nothing to do with Fiske, with his uncle's business, with all the increasing nightmares around them.

"So," she said. "We're stuck on a boat with a murderer. This is so not what I had in mind when I took this job. And Ivan being sick isn't helping anything, either.... Uh-oh." She glanced up, caught the expression on his face. "What else is wrong?"

"I hate boats." He balanced between the counters, but he could feel it—how the wind had picked up. The boat was sloshing from side to side. He couldn't fathom how she could continue to cook. Even more, he couldn't imagine why tumultuous seas didn't bother her.

"Are you going to turn green on me, Harm?"

He shook his head. "I don't get seasick. I just hate boats."

"I'll bet you only hate things you can't control or fix on your own, right?"

"Are you insulting me again?" But he was immediately diverted when he saw her open a bottle of liquor and pour it liberally into a saucepan. "You take up drinking while cooking? Not that I'm against it."

"Actually, no, although this would sure be a good day for it. The dessert's called Yukon Bread Pudding because it has some liberal Yukon Jack liquor in the sauce."

"What kind of liquor is that?"

"Trust me. You won't care when you taste it." Possibly because this day, like yesterday and the day before, had been exhaustingly traumatic, she suddenly zipped across the galley, pounced up on her toes and planted a good, solid kiss right on his open mouth.

He had no chance to react before she was back to whisking cream and butter into the Yukon Jack on the stove.

He rubbed a hand over his jaw. "Did I just dream that?"

"Uh-huh. It never happened," she assured him.

The response in her eyes, though, wasn't teasing but... warning. The two of them had a reckoning coming. It had nothing to do with murder and mayhem, and conceivably might be even more earth-shattering than murder and mayhem, anyway.

At least for him.

Maybe for her, too. She stirred the whiskey so hard it almost sloshed out of the pan.

The sound of the intercom startled them both. Harm

was being paged to the pilothouse, where Hans's voice relayed there was a message for him.

"Damn," he murmured.

"That's what I was thinking," she murmured right back.

But he had to go.

Chapter 9

An hour later, Cate was a pinch away from putting dinner on, and mentally yelling at herself for stupidity. Dinner had turned into an award-winning feast, which was ridiculous. She'd created way, way too much to do for a woman recovering from a nasty headache and major bruises.

In the next life, she was going to *learn*. She was going to be smarter. And for damn sure, she was going to have good hair.

She carted plates and silverware to the dining room, then went back to her galley. She glanced at the clock, thinking she had just enough time to hustle down to the crew quarters, and make sure the captain was still alive. Her last trip below, Ivan had yelled that he was dying and anyone who bugged him would die with him—which seemed a good sign. If he was strong enough to yell, he couldn't be too bad off.

She stirred, checked, piled used pots into the dishwasher, opened wine to breathe, pulled the herbed tomatoes from the oven. On the intercom, she heard Hans. "Some rough weather building," he warned her. "Shouldn't get here for another three hours, but then we'll all want to batten down the hatches, get things sealed up tight. Afraid it's going to slow up our return run into Juneau."

"You need help, you just say," Cate said. "You out of coffee up there?"

"Don't need coffee, but I'm sure hungry."

"It'll be ready in another twenty," she promised. Maybe all her flying around wasn't such a bad idea. She couldn't dwell on her hurts, on obsessing about who had pushed her last night, on fear for her life. Fear for Harm. Fear *of* Harm. Damn it. She'd escaped falling in love for twenty-nine years, so how could it possibly happen in less than a week's time?

Falling in love just wasn't in her game plan.

Yet her heart sprinted the instant she saw Harm, his face and jacket splashed from the temper-prone sea. He had his hand on the door to her galley when he was interrupted. Yale had just walked into the dining room. Harm changed course and entered the side door into the dining area.

Cate told herself to quit mooning and concentrate. She tasted, almost burning her tongue. It wasn't easy to get the exact ratios of horseradish and Tabasco and Worcestershire sauce and onion and lime just right.

For darn sure she didn't have time to eavesdrop…but it wasn't her fault that voices carried clearly from the open dining area.

From the sound, she suspected Yale had just poured himself something to drink from the liquor cabinet. "I didn't think I'd get a chance to talk to you alone," he said to Harm. "Everyone's going to be coming up for dinner, so maybe this isn't the time, either. But I've got something to say."

"So go for it," Harm encouraged him quietly.

"I found Arthur going through my stuff. And if you want the truth, I went through Purdue's things when we first got here. This is killing us all. We're turning into animals instead of the team players we used to be. I need to be cleared of this. So I want you to…"

"What?"

"I want to give you access to my bank accounts, my personal records, everything. I want you to investigate me. I want you to verify that I haven't come into any sudden wealth, that I have no change in circumstance. I'll sign anything you want, to give you permission to find out anything you need to about me."

Cate held her breath, wanting to hear Harm's answer… only she couldn't. The risotto cakes had turned crisp and she still had to prepare the last-minute dishes. She carted dinner up to Hans in the pilothouse, checked one last time on Ivan below—who was still only communicating in swear-speak—then started to serve.

By then, Arthur and Purdue had joined the group. There was no joking at dinner about anyone falling in love with her. They ate. In fact, they devoured everything she put in front of them, which should have fed an entire platoon. Several times, Harm ordered her to sit down and relax and eat herself.

Several times, she tried.

Outside, clouds had blown in, darkened the sky, started pitching rain, which only added to the gloomy mood of the guys.

"We need to go *home*," Yale kept saying.

And that became the general mantra. As soon as they got home, everything would be better, they'd figure it all out, they'd do this, they'd do that. Arthur suggested publicly at dinner the same thing Yale had cornered Harm about just an hour before.

"I've thought relentlessly about the disappearance and loss of our project," he said to Harm. "And I think one thing you need to do…you must do…is look into all of our circumstances. Check out financial records. Our homes. Whatever you need to do to make all of us more transparent."

"I already offered that," Yale said.

"I'm not hot to have anyone in my private life," Purdue said uncomfortably. "But you can look at my finances and taxes and all that crap for sure."

Several times, her gaze locked with Harm, even though she was running around between the galley and dining room. But the conversation seemed extraordinary, considering someone had to be guilty of theft—and likely murder and assault, as well. All of them sounded so innocent. All them appeared more than willing to prove there'd been no financial or any other kind of gain or change in their lives.

Only the formula was gone.

And Fiske was dead.

And she'd been pushed off the top deck.

And now Ivan was sick as a dog—maybe not poisoned, but it seemed beyond coincidental that a man with a cast-iron stomach would suddenly get ill, particularly because his illness proved to be a catalyst, the one thing that guaranteed they'd all call off the trip and head for home.

After dinner, Harm announced he was going up to the pilothouse. "Hans must be exhausted. I don't know when he plans to drop anchor for the night, but I'll spell him until he chooses to hang it up. If the captain's still sick tomorrow, I think we should all take turns."

Everyone agreed to that. By the time she'd sanitized the galley, the ship was pitching and tossing. The guys all claimed they were turning in early. She checked on Ivan one more time, then headed below deck to her claustrophobic cabin.

Internet connection was sporadic, but she still managed to connect with both sisters. Startling her no end, there were a series of notes from both. Who is this Harm? demanded Sophie several times, and Lily echoed the same kind of comments. You never mentioned a guy since I can remember. Call immediately when you get back on dry land.

Cate couldn't remember saying a word about Harm. Weirder yet, her sisters must have forgotten that she was the caretaker and question-asker, the nosy one who watched out for the two of them—not the other way around.

She didn't need watching over.

After turning off the computer, she stared at the wild seas through her porthole...and then moved. There was something she still needed to do tonight. Something more important than anything she'd done in a long, long time.

Possibly it took some traumatic accidents and disasters to make her rethink about what really mattered.

Harm prowled the circumference of the boat one last time—a pretty senseless thing to do in the rain, but he couldn't rest. Everyone had long gone below, holed up in their cabins like squirrels on a dark winter day. He'd spoken with Ivan, gotten his own key to the pilothouse so he could continue sending and receiving messages through the night. It was still late afternoon in Cambridge, so it was possible more information could still come through from home base.

He'd accumulated information from the radio tonight nonstop. He had information and evidence of all kinds coming out of the woodwork—but nothing that had settled his mind. He'd never needed their permission to investigate his three men, but the P.I. firm he'd hired had dusted every closet in their lives.

None of them appeared guilty of anything. He'd found a few unpaid parking tickets. Years before, Arthur was guilty of a personal indiscretion when he'd been briefly separated from his wife. Yale and Purdue had smoked a few funny cigarettes in their college years. Purdue's father had kicked his son around, causing a divorce and likely some scars on Purdue's soul.

But there wasn't one thing to indicate all three men weren't bright, decent men who'd primarily been honest most of their lives. Certainly there was nothing pointing to guilt—much less guilt of the dangerous, reckless crimes going on.

Harm hated intrusively prying into their lives, and by the time he went below, he was damp-cold and his head was buzzing from exhaustion and stress. He hadn't slept, really slept, since before his uncle died, or that's how it felt. His neck was stiffer than dried rope, his eyes gritty.

His intent was to crash, long and hard—but not until he'd checked on Cate. She'd been on his mind nonstop, above, beyond and below anything else going on. Still, first he needed to stop at his cabin. Just hiking around the boat had given him a cold dose of wet sea, so he figured he'd drop off his wet jacket and shoes in his cabin before knocking on hers.

He unlocked his door, and before even stepping in, sensed immediately that something was odd.

He closed the door, stood still. No sound intruded in the silence. The Alaskan eternal twilight should have provided more ambient light, even this late, but the gloomy rain clouds had darkened the skies. His cabin was a muzzy charcoal, wasn't going to get better until his eyes adjusted.

Quietly, he peeled off his wet jacket and heeled off his deck shoes, every sense still on red alert, trying to identify the "something" that was off. The instinct of danger overwhelmed his senses, hitched his breathing. After everything that had happened, he was prepared for anything. Or he told himself he was.

But it seemed…his gaze narrowed as his vision finally adjusted to the darkness…it seemed that his accelerated heart rate was responding to an entirely different kind of danger than any he could have anticipated. The "odd" thing, he identified, was the lump in his bed. The small, long lump under the blankets.

Slowly, he reached for his belt, unlatched it.

"If that's Goldilocks," he said lowly, "I'm not sure if you're in the right bed." The pants followed the belt to the floor; then he yanked the pullover over his head. "Were you looking for the big bear, the medium bear or the just right bear?"

"It is Goldilocks, and I'm only interested in the big bear." The voice was as small as the body.

"Well, damn. You've got the right one then."

But he wasn't totally up for joking, even as he lifted the first layer of sheet and blanket and slid in. She shrieked, not the most seductive sound he'd ever heard. Possibly his skin struck her as ice-cold, at least compared to her nice, warm body. But he wasn't actually trying to lay hands on her, only to tuck her in tight around the neck, make sure there were no air leaks.

"Listen, Ms. Trouble. I want you here. I want you sleeping here, because it's a better bed, and I know you're safe, and I want you next to me. But that's it. You were not only hurt, you put out another 500 percent day. You need rest. And you're going to get it."

She edged up on an elbow, undoing all that meticulous

tucking and safekeeping he'd done. "Yeah, right," she murmured, and then pounced.

He was going to mention that he'd never met a woman he couldn't seduce. He was going to also add that even his ex-wives never had a complaint about his lovemaking. That he'd always taken the lead, because he was damned good at taking charge—and taking charge of giving a woman pleasure was one of his favorite skills. Furthermore, women liked it slow. Which he knew. And catered to.

But my God. He couldn't get anything said. Hell. He couldn't even get a thought to stick in his head long enough to consider saying it.

She swarmed him—took him over, took him under—with warm, liquid kisses. With hands that kneaded and teased and took. Her hands seemed intent on learning any and everything that could conceivably rile him beyond sanity.

Brazen fingers strayed over his chest, then down, past his abdomen, finally closing over him as if she owned him, which at that moment, she did, lock stock and barrel. She squeezed tight, then stroked and explored some more. Above ground zero, a brazen tongue discovered his Adam's apple, his earlobe, his mouth, after which she took her kisses lower. Those lips of hers snaked down at the same speed as her hands.

She disappeared under the covers.

Not a good sign.

Harm was beyond worried—about his good men, about his one rotten apple. About her. About trouble he'd brought on this boat. About Fiske. About failing his uncle and his uncle's legacy.

But for the first time in hours, in days—possibly in his entire life—he could allow some of that responsibility to slip.

Conceivably, he didn't really have a choice.

She took him in. Some way, somehow, for him she kept turning into the eternal woman. He knew that was idiotic thinking, but that was the whole range of emotions she invoked in him. Everything was about her and her boundless capacity for giving, for feeling, for being.

Like now. She teased him with her mouth, her tongue, her fingertips. Then twisted around before he could retaliate, and rubbed against him, with her breasts, her pelvis. She laughed with her low throaty whisper...then tickled a fingernail down his ribs...then slicked up his torso with her whole body like a cuddling cat...then sat on him, straddling his hips, weaving side to side, feeling the heavy hard shape of him, but not just joining. Just offering an engraved invitation. Over and over.

Until he'd had it.

She knew how to get a man in a rage, that was for damn sure.

By the time he scooped her beneath him, he didn't know or care what his own name was, didn't care if he lost everything he owned, didn't care if he never had another thing. As long as he could have her. Then. Right then.

Yet he impaled her with a tender, slow slide, wanting

both of them to feel the possession, the possibilities. The soar from there clutched them both...then set them free.

She called his name on a long, soft sigh, both of them holding tight long before the spasms of pleasure had eased. Finally, he sank back, pulling her on top of him. Her skin was as slick as his, her breathing as ragged as his.

He smiled, even in the darkness. And kissed her until she dropped off into a deep sleep.

In the middle of the night, he found her curled around him like a scarf, draped every which way, tucked up everywhere she could touch. Yet she suddenly reared up on her elbows, and said out of nowhere, "No."

"No what?" Apparently, he'd been stroking her back, just a light caress, nothing that was meant to wake or trouble her.

"No, you're not going to have insomnia tonight. You think I wasted all that energy and effort seducing you just so you could spend another night worrying? How are you going to think if you don't get some rest? Now that's it. Go to sleep."

"I think it's possible," he marveled, "that the only bossier person than you...happens to be me."

Her cheek nuzzled back against his shoulder. "Don't divert the issue. Suck it up and go to sleep."

"You think you seduced me, huh?"

"I know I did." Her voice was very sleepy, very smug.

He tried to understand it—how he could conceivably have fallen in love with such an impossible, contrary woman. She was full of herself and irrepressible and listened to no one. She was a hopelessly free spirit.

He was completely the opposite.

It was easy to recognize their differences. It was impossibly hard to believe he'd never see her again, once they landed in Juneau.

Murder and mayhem were cupcake-size problems by comparison.

Being with Cate was a problem he had to solve—before it was too late.

Cate slipped out of bed while Harm was still sleeping. She tiptoed from the room, carrying her clothes, determined not to wake him. She knew how exhausted he had to be. After a fast shower, she headed top deck.

She could see Hans had already pulled anchor, was installed in the pilothouse, sailing full bore toward Juneau. She popped open the door. "You need coffee?"

"I'd die for a cup," he said. "How's the head and bruises?"

"Colorful. And I confess I'm creaking a little this morning." She was stiff, so darned if she could imagine why her mood was sky-high. "Do we know how Ivan is?"

"Mad as a hornet. I don't know what got to him. If I didn't know better, I'd say he took an emetic. He looked a shade paler than death this morning, but he's alive. Tried to get up. Couldn't. I do think he'll be all right, but don't think we'll see him for a while yet."

She chatted with Hans a little longer, but then aimed

below. Both Hans and Arthur were her early coffee cravers, and once the urn was set to brew, she started on breakfast. Scotch eggs this morning, she thought. Something easy.

At least easy on her terms. Before six, her galley had turned into a production line. The sausage, onion and fresh sage were in one bowl. The stuffing crumbs in another. The flour set up to dip the peeled hard-boiled eggs into. She was humming some silly blues tune when she suddenly whipped around and saw Harm in the doorway.

His blond head was still damp from a shower, his sweatshirt almost—*almost*—as frayed and old as her own. He was leaning against the doorjamb as if he'd been watching her for some time, his mouth tilted in a lazy smile.

"Hey," he murmured.

"Hey right back." Something clutched in her stomach, something tight and sharp and unexpected. She'd say it was fear; she hadn't felt fear—real fear—since the fire when she was a kid. Still, this was that same sensation of watching her life spin out of control, risking the loss of everything, unable to stop it.

She wanted to be there for Harm. To see that light in his eyes every morning.

It was the scariest thing she could remember. And then he started talking.

"I have a favor to ask you."

"Shoot." She pulled out two frying pans, measured the oil.

"I need your help. So I want you to come home with

me." Before she could answer, he said, "Now don't say no without hearing me out."

"I'm listening. But only for two seconds. No more."

He started talking, his tone all lazy and easy—on the surface. "When we get back home, the mystery's still waiting, nothing solved, nothing right. Every bit of information seems to lead to more dead ends. I need your eyes, your perspective, your ears. I'll be completely alone when I go back to Cambridge—I've got a team of lawyers, a firm of private investigators. But I only moved there a few weeks back, so there's no one who's close to me. No one I can trust."

"You're getting that tone in your voice. That I-can-seduce-you tone. Forget it. I have to earn a living, remember? I can't just go off gallivanting anytime and anywhere I want."

"I thought you could. And did."

She frowned, started slicing tomatoes for a garnish, almost nipped her finger. "Well, actually, I do. But I still have to earn a—"

"Yeah, I heard you. But do you have an immediate chef job lined up after this?"

"Not immediate, no. I've got the next gig lined up, but I have to have a space of time between to pay my bills, regroup, plan ahead. The Internet's my office, how I find and set up jobs, initially. And if I hit a dry spell… which usually happens a couple weeks in a year…then I hit on one of my chef friends I know from New Orleans, hang out in their kitchens. It might sound a little…well, braggy. But a good chef can always pull down good money. Even for short-term gigs."

"That would only sound braggy to someone who hasn't tasted your cooking."

Her eyes narrowed again. "Don't you start with that tone again. I don't do sweet-talking."

"I know, Cookie. You're tough. But the question is whether you're pinned down for the next couple weeks."

"Not exactly," she said firmly.

"In other words, no. So here's the deal. I'll pay your flight, your expenses, a wage." He named a figure that made her choke. In fact, she had to lean forward, while he helpfully thumped her on the back to get her over it.

"Don't be ridiculous," she gasped.

"I need help. Your help. I'm willing to pay for it."

"Look, hotshot. I can be bought. It's easy. But that's an insane amount of money. Period."

"Everyone's in a hurry to get home, Cate. There has to be a reason. Something's there, in the lab, something the one guilty party is worried about. Something the investigators haven't caught, that I haven't caught, that the whole team working together after my uncle died couldn't see. I need a fresh set of eyes. More relevant, I need *your* eyes. Because I trust you, and because you've already shown me that you are perceptive about people and situations."

She could feel herself start to relent, which was crazy. She was smarter than that. "What I know about science wouldn't fill a thimble."

"Join the club. The core of this mystery, I've become convinced, isn't about knowledge. They all had the same knowledge. It's about something that doesn't belong. Something that's been hidden. Something that needs to strike one of us as out of place."

"Really, I can't."

"It wouldn't be for long. I figure we'll be in Cambridge no later than three days from now. Late Friday night'd be the soonest, if we can book flights and arrangements all work out. If we've got a chance of finding something, I believe it's got to be this weekend—before everyone shows up on Monday, and the culprit has another chance to cover his tracks."

"Really, Harm. I can't." In the dining room, she heard sounds…probably Arthur, pouring his first cup of joe. And then Purdue. Both of them started talking, then went up on deck.

Harm picked up the argument the instant they were out of earshot. "The police have been all over the place, found nothing. And there'll be a funeral I'll need to attend, for Fiske. My absence will be another occasion for the culprit to hide his tracks. So we've only got a short time where there's a shot at getting to the bottom of this. And you're the only one who can help me."

"Harm, are you deaf? I can't!"

"I'd worry if you said yes easily," he admitted. "You've already been hurt. The last thing I want is to risk putting you in any more danger. The problem, though, is that our guilty guy could think you know something, which is likely why he pushed you off the deck to begin with. And if he's smart enough to pull off everything else he has, from theft to hiding something so massive and protected, to possibly murder and definitely hurting you—then he'll sure as hell be smart enough to track you down, wherever you are. So, I think you're safer with me than alone. That we'll both be safer if we stick together until this is resolved."

For the first time since early yesterday, her head screamed like a banshee. "You're so slick. You think you can talk anybody into anything," she said disgustedly.

"Only for my girl."

"I'm not your girl. And just for the record, I'm not falling in love with you!" She whirled around, just in time to see Arthur and Yale standing patiently at the end of the doorway.

"We were just going to ask about breakfast," Yale said guilelessly.

"Out! All of you! Out!"

Yale shot out of sight. Then Arthur. Harm turned around, too, carrying the two dishes she handed him to put on the table—but he still didn't leave until he'd dropped a kiss on top of her head.

"Last night," he said, "you took my heart."

Then he left. After doing that same thing that roiled up her stomach and igniting the same miserable fight-flight instinct again.

Chapter 10

When the jet bounced down onto the tarmac at Logan Airport, Harm was buzz-tired. Making sudden travel arrangements meant all of them had been on different flights, different times, and never, for damn sure, conveniently. He'd managed to keep Cate with him all the way, but they'd still been traveling for two nonstop days, with meals on the run, and layovers in airports that all looked alike.

He'd never been able to sleep on planes, partly because he was prone to insomnia and primarily because the seats were made for midgets. Cate, by contrast, had zoned out each time an engine started and slept like the dead, mostly sprawled on him. Now, she galloped down the aisle, all perky and bossy.

She started out with, "You and I are going to have a serious talk. About what I'm really doing here."

"You know why you're here."

"Humph."

She went along with those humphs until right before the baggage claim escalators, where she stopped all passenger flow by stopping dead and wagging a finger in his face. "I'll help you if I can. That's not even an issue. But you and I both know what's really going on here. You want to be with me. I want to be with you. We're having temporary delusions that we've something mystical and fantastic and rare and extraordinary going on together."

"And this is criminal how?" he asked carefully.

She didn't answer that. Someone bumped her, and she charged off toward baggage claim again. "This is just not planned out well. I don't have any clothes, for one thing. For Pete's sake, all I carried with me were the clothes I needed for a boat trip in Alaska."

"Doesn't seem that hard to use a credit card in a store, does it?"

"I hate shopping," she informed him.

"I knew you would," he said mildly. Somehow, even with no rest, his eyes gritty from dryness, and Armageddon waiting for him at the lab, he felt as relaxed as a sleepy lion. It was Cate. Everything she'd said was true. Everything about his feelings for her were suspect and not to be trusted and, well, odd. Odd for him, anyway.

No man felt sure of a woman. Certainly, no man after two divorces felt sure of a woman—much less one as capricious and unreadable as Cate.

But there it was. The feeling that anything was

solvable when she was next to him. That nothing would ever be right again if she wasn't.

She fell silent for a brief—very brief—stretch, while they picked up their gear and made the trek to the long-term parking lot. The weather was a mighty contrast to the damp greens of Alaska. The late-afternoon sky sun-bleached and summer heat baked into the pavement. In the car lot, once he'd given her the general location, he had to chuckle when she instinctively aimed for a black BMW 128i convertible.

"How on earth could you guess which was my car?"

"It's obvious. Look at the rest of the cars in this row—the Taurus and Chevy and Mazdas. But don't try telling me you bought it because it's a precision driving machine."

"It is."

"It's also the sexiest BMW they ever put out. How fast can you get that top down?"

"You're a good woman, Cate. Forget all the insults I said before."

She rolled her eyes, but she was getting it back—that irrepressible grin. "We'd better quit with the chitchat. Do we have a plan? Besides your needing to clock in some serious hours of sleep."

"I don't need sleep."

"Harm. You're going to crash, soon and big. You have to have some rest."

Maybe he did, but Harm figured he'd have to manage. He knew the other men's travel schedules. Come Monday morning, latest, everybody would be back to work at the lab. That left him the weekend, at most, for him and Cate to take that place apart from stem to stern.

It wasn't likely to be enough time.

Even so, he had priorities before that. It felt good to slide behind the wheel, get the top off, put his baby in gear. There weren't that many miles between Logan and Cambridge, but it was Friday, approaching rush hour, so naturally the roads were jammed. Rather than face Interstate 93, he ducked down the side roads around Harvard.

Truthfully, he could have found a better route than that, but he wanted Cate to get a glimpse of Harvard Square, the white-spired churches, the historical streets with the red brick and white trim and black lanterns. Big old shade trees cooled the side streets, showed off small, elegant gardens, history hiding in every side corner.

"You like?" he asked, but he could tell from the way she absorbed it all.

"Totally love," she corrected him.

"Yeah, that's how I felt when I first got here. I don't know the entire region that well yet. And traffic in Boston—there's no swear word bad enough to describe it. But still…the whole area's been growing on me."

"New Orleans was like that for me. I first went because of the fantastic chefs located there. It's impossible in the summer, not just hot, but sick-hot. Still, there's so much character and flavor in the city that it was easy to fall in love with." She turned to him. "You still haven't told me the plan."

"Because I don't have anything that specific." There was a lot on his mind, but for long minutes, he'd just been aware of the summer wind in their faces, tossing up her hair, her riding next to him, how nothing had felt this easy or right in a long time. Maybe never. "First plan. We need to drop our bags off at my place. Both of us probably want to catch a shower. Then—out for a decent dinner. Too late to get reservations at a place like the Barking Crab restaurant, but I know a good place locally. So...we'll freshen up, eat, then drive over to the lab. I don't know that we can get much of anything done tonight, but we can at least map out our time from there."

"Good plan. One small exception."

"What?"

"I need clothes. Seriously. Nothing fancy, but I just need some kind of generic store where I could pick up a few basics—specifically clothes that don't smell like fish and rain."

"No sweat." He immediately right-turned, aimed a few blocks into a more commercial area. A man couldn't have been married, much less twice, without knowing about women and clothes shopping, so...she was going to take forever. He really didn't care. Actually, he figured he could swing into a shady spot and put his head back, catch a nap. Even a half hour would be better than none.

He pulled onto a commercial street with a half dozen decent shops, angled into a parking spot, then lifted up to pull out his wallet and a credit card.

She shot him a look that could have frozen fire. "Have I neglected to mention that I make damn good money and certainly don't need yours?"

"But I said I'd pay for expenses. And you wouldn't need these clothes if I didn't push you into helping me."

"Do not irritate me when I have jet lag, Connolly. Trust me. It's a bad idea. It's possible you're right, because it sort of is an expense. But I don't care. I buy my own clothes. That's that."

He wiped a hand over his face as she climbed out and clipped down the street, but then he just put his head back and closed his eyes with a grin. How—or why—a completely irrational woman should make him smile was impossible to analyze.

A second later—certainly no more—she was climbing back in the car with four packages. He blinked in shock. "You just left." He glanced at his watch. "You haven't even been fifteen minutes."

"I easily fit in a size. And the first store was great, hit a sale. Home, Jerome."

Abruptly, he remembered a few details. "It's not actually home. It was my uncle's place. I haven't had time to sell it, or do much of anything for that matter. He died, I got here, and the whole crisis of the disappearing formula developed from there. So I—"

"So it's dusty and messy. Got it, Harm. You're talking to a woman who doesn't claim anywhere as home. You don't need to worry about stuff like that with me. Ever."

"I'm not worried. I'm just trying to warn you what we're getting into." To himself, Harm admitted that he had an attachment to the place. Not that he wouldn't sell it. Not that it didn't need work to accommodate how he'd prefer to live. It was just…growing up, Dougal had been his favorite family person. He wasn't just an uncle but a coconspirator, someone a cocky boy could talk to— about girls, about life, about building a windmill in the backyard, about sort of accidentally driving his mom's car into the ditch a week after he got his license.

So. It wasn't that the house was so much. It's just that he wanted her to like it.

When they pulled up she looked it over, said "Really nice" in a tone that told him nothing at all, then started grabbing her packages and duffel. "Point me to a shower, okay?"

He unlocked, carried and then obediently pointed. "Wander anywhere you want. I'll be in—" He pointed again, this time across a hall "—that shower. I'm going to make a few calls first, okay? Make yourself at home."

He did have calls to make. The airlines, to make sure what times Arthur, Yale and Purdue were expected home—which was not for another day. After that, he called Fiske's daughter, then checked answering-machine messages and left callbacks for the firm's attorney and the P.I. firm. He didn't expect responses—not on Friday night—but he still wanted the host of players involved in his uncle's firm to be aware that he was home and needed further updating.

His firm, Harm kept telling himself. All of it was his problem now, not his uncle's.

By the time he hung up, he realized he hadn't heard a sound from Cate. The bathroom door was closed where he'd directed her—which was the spare bath, had clean towels and no guy-messes that he could remember.

He headed for his own shower, and before he'd gotten the first layer of travel grime off, he was trying to imagine the house through her eyes.

It was just a basic brownstone type. Grown-in neighborhood, all ages. The yard backed up to woods and a ravine, but it wasn't fancy, looked more like a professor's digs than a millionaire's dream house. Practically every room had bookshelves. The main living area had big, fat furniture, either old leather or corduroy, with splashes of dark red and blues in the Oriental carpets. Three bedrooms, a dining room no one had ever used to eat in, a den that was piled to the ceiling. There were no doodads, but dust coming off the books scented the air.

By the time he'd toweled off, nicked his chin twice shaving, and climbed into pants, he figured she'd hate it...but he couldn't wait any longer before finding her. He pulled on a white shirt, thinking about dinner, but was still buttoning it as he started the search.

It was still hot—the house had been closed up, obviously—and he'd put on AC when he called the restaurant, but it was going to take a while to get the place cooled down. He padded barefoot into the living room. A window seat in the bay windows looked onto the two giant maples in the front yard. A black squirrel was perched on the windowsill, as if he owned the place. It was the one room that had some coolness to it, he thought, but that wasn't where he found Cate.

She was standing in the middle of the kitchen,

wearing a short silk wrap, a hairbrush in her hand. It didn't appear as if she'd used it yet. Her hair glistened, still damp from a shower, and was standing up in spiky enthusiasm. Typical of Cate, when she concentrated, she forgot everything else.

He edged up behind her, folded his arms. "What exactly are we looking at?" he asked.

She jumped when she realized he was there, then grinned. She motioned to where he saw an old box of a kitchen, a broom closet, a sturdy but well-scarred oak table. Last time someone had given the room attention, they'd gone for blue. It was definitely the most neglected room in the house, yet Cate's face radiated animation and delight.

"I love a kitchen with an east view. That long sill is just a natural for growing herbs. The broom closet's kind of a silly waste, but if you look at the space inside, it wouldn't take much work to create a really convenient pantry. And the sink. I love a serious double sink. And that's a great work counter. Personally, I think it needs better lighting, and obviously a paint job, but the guts of a terrific kitchen is already here. You can't imagine how rare that is. I—"

She didn't stop talking until he pulled her into his arms.

"What?" she asked, on the cusp of a laugh.

"You. Orgasmic over a kitchen. An old, beat-up, ugly kitchen."

"It's a little beat-up, but that isn't the point—"

"I know." Her excitement was the point. Which was why he had to kiss her. It had been aeons. She'd slept half in his arms on the flights, but there'd been no privacy for days, for exhausting, long hours. Being next to her was good. Very good.

But it wasn't the same as finally getting his hands on her.

He didn't know he'd been holding back and behaving himself until he tasted her lips again. That silky small mouth was as sassy as her personality, teasing and tasting and then settling in for a long, lingering savor. Her tongue got into it, then her teeth.

Her arms slid around his neck, clung. She swayed against him, deliberately giving him a tease of pelvis, a brush of breast. All promises, no substance.

She was not a good woman. Not a fair one. But she let out a wicked, low chuckle when he brushed something off the table—paper? Mail? Whatever. He needed a mattress and the only bed-type was far too many yards away.

"We don't have time," she murmured. "Didn't you say we were going to dinner—?"

"Reservations. In an hour. Don't care."

"I thought you were starving."

"I am."

"We have serious stuff to do. We really don't have time—"

This from the woman who was helping him swoosh mail and newspapers and keys to the floor, who'd already perched up on the table, who was sliding her hands inside his white shirt.

She was totally right. They didn't have time.

For anything but this.

The chaos of the last two days disappeared. The wild sail back to Juneau, the jumbled flight and transfer arrangements, the chaotic connections with authorities at home and in Juneau—it had all been never ending, nonstop. Until now. With her.

Those small white hands handled the zipper on his dress pants so fast, he was ready to go, and there she was, laughing, coaxing him with more kisses, more speed. Her legs wrapped around him, bringing him closer, at the same time her tongue whisked damp, soft enticements down his throat, his chest, lower.

He put a stop to it.

She'd seduced him once, but the darned woman needed to learn to take turns. When she heard him laugh, she lifted her head, smiled up at him. "See, Harm?" she whispered. "That's the thing. To steal moments of feeling good and being happy and just…being. With someone else. Just…"

Oh, yeah, now she wanted to talk? He hooked her legs under his arms, lifted them up and over his shoulders. He took his turn—and he made it a slow, long, lazy turn—whisking his tongue down, down, starting with the hollow in her ivory-soft throat. Then celebrating the shape and vulnerability and exquisite texture of each small, perfect breast. Then down, over her flat tummy, into her navel.

"Harm…" There, he saw her head drop back. She wasn't laughing anymore. There was still a smile, but it was fragile, stark, intimate. "I don't think I can…"

Yeah, he thought. That was the thing. She wasn't a truster—which he understood, because he trusted no one, either. But that was exactly how he knew what to do, why, how. For her to believe that she could give her trust to him, he had to come through for her.

A man dreamed of work this good. His tongue dipped lower, lower, until he cupped his hands under her bottom, lifted her to him and sipped. She let out a cry of a sigh, a moan of longing and need. He tasted, savored, sank in.

She arched under his hands, then tensed until he felt the first vibrant tremors take her over, take her under. Before she'd recovered, he rewound her legs, this time around his waist, and plunged into her, hard and slow.

She called his name again, but this time on a hiss. The sound inspired him to dive deeper, slower, harder. They both seemed to crest on a roar of speed, a thrill of letting free…everything. For her. With her.

Moments later, they were both gasping for breath. "What you do to me," she whispered, half laughing, half scolding, her tone so loving he almost lost it all over again. Unfortunately, they had to separate—the table was impossibly uncomfortable; both had to shift. And reality, of course, returned. They still had miles to travel in the coming hours.

Harm, though, figured he'd get more recovery time, because when she disappeared in the bedroom, he figured she'd take a lot longer than he would to get dressed and fixed up. Instead, he'd barely caught a fast reshower and changed and had a chance to sit in a living-room chair before she walked out of the spare bedroom.

At first, he thought a stranger had broken into the house and done something with his Cate.

It was just a black dress, he could see. But she'd done something with a scarf, added a little vanilla and dark chocolate in a low scoop under her neck. The heels were so high she almost reached his chin, not counting how long and sexy they made her legs look. Her hair was still a wreck, thank God, so at least he could recognize her. But the eyes looked smoky and dangerous, something tiny and expensive dangling from her ears.

"Who are you and what have you done with my Cate?"

She walked by him, chucked up his chin. "Didn't you think I could clean up? But don't start thinking I'd be any kind of corporate wife. I don't do country clubs. Or private schools. Or being on boards."

"But I'll bet you do expensive restaurants."

She brightened immediately. "I *can* be bought. That's my price. Where are you taking me?"

"Nowhere around men if you're going to wear those heels and look like that. Hell, I need oxygen before I can find the strength to drive the car."

"Damn it, Harm. You go straight to my head. Cut it out."

He didn't want to cut it out. He strongly suspected she wasn't normally into blushing, and his ego thrived on flustering her.

The drive wasn't far, and he put the car on zoom, because both of them really were hungry and needed a decent meal. He admitted wanting to impress her, and he knew she'd like the restaurant. He'd been there twice. He couldn't pronounce a thing on the menu, but everything went down easy. It was in an old house, each room uniquely decorated, but all had subtle lighting and long, graceful drapes and restful chairs.

The waiter offered them a wine list, then the menu— which Cate, with a glance at Harm, suggested they didn't really need. "How about if you just bring us whatever the chef thinks is his favorite tonight?"

The older man smiled. "He'll love that. And I think you will, too."

This might be the only peaceful meal they'd have for days, Harm thought, and it was going to be perfect.

That illusion lasted maybe three minutes.

"Okay," she said, after the first sip of wine, "maybe it's time you told me about those first two wives."

"Now you want to hear? I've offered a half dozen times."

"You don't have to tell me if you don't want to. I just figured we'd have a more restful dinner if we didn't talk about murder and larceny and all that for a little while."

He was more than willing to tell her. "The first one was Zoe. We got married the day after my eighteenth birthday. She was pregnant. Neither of us had a brain, crossed state lines, found a justice of the peace, figured we'd somehow work it all out and conquer the world. We were 100 percent in love. Never doubted for a minute our love could endure anything—including her parents' disapproval and mine."

"So what tore it apart?"

"Not parents. Not poverty. Not idiocy. But...she

miscarried in her sixth month. It tore us both up. I guess that has to sound pretty nuts for an eighteen-year-old kid to want a baby that bad. But I did. Anyway, neither of us had the maturity to survive the loss, at least not together, because we both caved after that. Nothing I'm proud to admit."

"Cripes, Harm. That's a sad story. What a thing to go through…." She suddenly shook her head.

"What?"

By then the waiter had served dinner with a flourish of sterling and bone china. Cate hadn't eaten two bites before she started in.

"The chef wouldn't know fresh cilantro if it knocked at his front door," she murmured. "And the wine's all right, although there are certainly better choices. So do you ever still see her? Zoe?"

"No. We stayed in touch for a while. Then that disappeared except for an e-mail at Christmas. She's been married for a while, on her third kid—I don't believe her husband even knows there was a marriage before him."

She had several more comments to make about dinner, but he wasn't deluded that she was finished grilling him. "Well, you might as well tell me about wife number two, since we started this. And I certainly hope that story is a lot more scandalous than the first one."

"Okay." He'd devoured his dinner by then. "I went to school after that. Liked engineering, but didn't like going to classes, that whole school environment. So I enlisted in the army. My dad thought that was crazy—I never owned a weapon, never wanted to, don't like anything about wars—but I seriously believed that career army was going to work for me. I didn't want to be an engineer who sat at a desk. I wanted to be one of those people who built bridges and roads and dams across the planet."

"And did you?"

"Oh, yeah. For years. Now what's wrong?" He saw the slight shake of her head.

"Nothing. I was just inclined for a second to go back to the kitchen and give the chef some friendly advice." She waved a fork. "Forget I said anything. You still haven't gotten into wife number two. Hard to imagine how a woman could have fit into that life program."

"Well, this wasn't exactly a typical marriage. In fact, what I'm about to tell you has a little tinge of not exactly kosher."

She shivered all over. "Good. Let's hear it." The dessert menu came and went. Some kind of fancy coffee was served, along with… Well, whatever it was tasted richer than Croesus.

"Kayla was Muslim. I met her in a hospital where I was getting stitches—not for anything interesting, just a minor accident, long cut on my side. Anyway. She was eighteen. A baby. So beat-up the doctors weren't sure she could survive it. I didn't see her initially—being a Muslim woman, she was treated only by females, and only behind closed curtains. But after I heard the story…I couldn't let it go. She was supposed to marry this man that she'd met, and strongly disliked. He was much older than she was. He told her up front what he expected in a wife. Her own father beat her when she claimed she couldn't marry him."

"My heavens," Cate murmured.

"She was suicidal. It wasn't just that she said it. I believed it. I think she would have killed herself if she had to go back to her family, to that 'fiancé.' So…"

"So you married her?"

"I know. That's the part that wasn't exactly kosher. Complicated as hell to pull off besides. There are too many people trying to immigrate to America, any way they can, so for a marriage to be 'valid', the pair has to stay together for a serious amount of time. She didn't have anyone here, didn't have any idea what to do with herself, her time, her life. All she wanted was to come to America, to get away from the situation she was in."

"How long did you stay married?"

Harm frowned, trying to remember. "First off, I got her in school—she was smart, just not educated in a system like ours. Thankfully, my family took to her, helped get her set up in a job after that, close enough they could be part of her world. I was still army then, still working projects around the world, so I couldn't be that close. But she thrived, almost from the start. It just took time to make it right, to make it work."

"Did you love her, Harm?"

"From the moment I first met her, I liked her. I cared about her. So, sure, I loved her."

"I mean, did you *love* love her?"

He answered the questions he figured she hadn't gotten around to asking yet. "I wasn't in love with anyone else. She was and is a terrific person. I honestly never regretted the marriage. I don't believe she did, either."

"But you did divorce."

He nodded. "She finally fell in love. But not with me. And to be honest—it was a relief, because I think she would have stayed with me out of loyalty and respect, and yeah, out of love. But not the right kind of love. Anyway, I still see her. She still sees my family. If I get you out to the left coast one of these days, you'll meet her, too. I guarantee you'll like her."

"Harm."

"What?"

"That was really a heroic thing to do!"

He frowned. "No, it wasn't. I wasn't with anyone else. I couldn't just walk away. I don't think anyone could have. I'm not exaggerating her situation. She would have died, and she had no possible way to help herself. Not in that culture." He cupped his chin in a hand. "You know, I was trying to treat you to a really nice dinner. You know. Like a date, even."

"This is a nice dinner! Thank you very much." Her voice radiated sincerity, although she did plunk down her spoon with a little distracted thunk. "Anyone can have a problem with cream. I'll bet he had an under chef handling the desserts, and he doesn't realize it's been overwhipped."

Harm shook his head. "Just so you know. If I ever want to seduce you or stage a romantic setting, I'm never taking you to a restaurant again. Maybe ever. It's a little too much like taking a cop to a robbery on his off day."

"What'd I do? What'd I say?" she asked bewilderedly.

"Nothing, Cookie. Now…you've got the story about my marriages out of me. Don't you think it's your turn to tell me about your guys?"

She blotted the corners of her mouth with a white linen napkin. "There've been millions. I can't remember them all."

"Ah. I believe that."

She glowered at him. "No, you don't."

Since they were putting a few straight cards on the table, he ventured a few more. "My guess is that there've been very few men…and none who you really loved. None who you really trusted. And since casual friends don't count, I'd guess the number is right around, well… one."

She blinked. "One?"

"Yeah. One. Me. You trust me, Cate."

She sucked in a breath. As he could have expected, she got that fight-or-flight look in her eyes again. Given a puff of wind, the scent of roses, the wrong kind of smile, she'd have bolted for the exit so fast it'd make his head spin.

But this time…she didn't bolt. She only looked as if she wanted to. "Don't flatter yourself, Connolly. But don't feel insulted, either. I don't trust anyone, not at a certain level. That's the way it is for me and always will be. I'm not the girl you take home. Trust me."

He'd already managed to take her home, Harm thought.

But not to win her. And for a man who had a full-scale trauma about to catch up with him, no time to even sleep, no way to keep her beyond a few more days… Harm was beginning to doubt there was any way he could force her to see what they were together.

What they could be.

Chapter 11

As they left the restaurant, Cate pulled her patience together and forced herself to say calmly, "Harm, you seriously need rest. I slept on the flights. You didn't. It just makes sense for you to get a few hours' sleep before we go to the lab."

Harm dug in his pocket for the car key. "I think it'd be a good idea for me to drop you off at the house. You catch some z's. I'll go to the lab."

Cate didn't kick him with one of her three-inch heels, but she was tempted. The man was more stubborn than a hound. He'd been cave-in tired by the time they'd finished dinner; she knew he couldn't keep going. But then his cell phone rang when he was paying the restaurant bill. She didn't know who called, only that he'd discovered Yale and Purdue had managed to catch an earlier flight.

None of the others were scheduled to arrive home before Sunday morning. Now, it appeared that two of them would be landing in Boston a full day earlier—as soon as fourteen hours from now.

"But," she reminded Harm, as he opened the passenger door for her, "they'll be exhausted. I'm sure they'll go to their own homes first, if only to drop off their gear and catch some rest. So we still likely have all day tomorrow before having to worry about them. And we'll get much more out of the day if you had some sleep."

"No."

That was all he said before closing her door. She simmered while he crossed the front of the car, climbed in, and started the engine. The problem with Harm, Cate had long realized, was that everyone had kowtowed to him for so long that he'd forgotten how to listen to anyone else. More relevant, no one had put a foot on his head and made him behave.

"Okay," she said sweetly. "This is the new plan. You said the lab was only a few miles from here, so we'll go there now. You can show me around, show me the whole setup. Then we'll go home. You get four hours' sleep. I'll wake you, we'll come back. In the meantime, you can call your security people and tell them no one's allowed in the lab without you getting a call."

Harm hesitated, and then admitted, "That's good thinking."

"But?"

"But...I'm going straight to the lab."

So, she mused. Next time she needed him to see

reason, she wouldn't waste time talking to him. She'd just hit him on the head with a baseball bat.

"I heard that," Harm mentioned.

"What?"

"You were mumbling. Loud enough for me to hear. This is the issue, Cate…you're safe while my men are still in the air. You're not safe once they land in Boston. So there's only one option here, and that's to find out everything I possibly can before they arrive. After that…"

"After that, what?"

He shot her a warm, possessive glance before returning his attention to the road. "After that, I'll figure out what I'm going to do about you."

"You might be strong, Harm, but it'll take more than you and an entire spare army to make me do anything I don't want to do." Her voice failed to pump up the volume she wanted to. Darn, it was hard to fight with him, partly because making crazy love with him on his kitchen table before dinner was still on her mind…and partly because of the way he kept looking at her.

She kept thinking about his ex-wives. She'd been so certain his divorce tales would be some version of today's usual horror story…two people who couldn't get along, who crucified each other in the divorce, who carried scars from the grief and the bitterness, who seemed to discover the worst of themselves and their chosen mates in the process.

She'd sort of expected that one marriage had to be a really young one—but not how warmly or honestly Harm had talked about that first love.

And she'd never imagined the scope of the second marriage, that he'd offer a ring to save a young woman's life. For Pete's sake, that was straight out of the archaic age of chivalry.

He was so adorable and so rich—and so arrogant—that she'd just assumed he was a player. Now…well… Cate sucked it up and figured she was stuck being nicer to him. At least to a point. "Well, you're not going to drive if you're overtired."

"Right on that. In fact, soon as we get to the lab, I'll give you the car keys. Then if you want to drive back to my place and crash, you can. Directions are easy."

True to his word, they were barely parked before he handed the keys to her. She climbed out of the car, nearly tripping on her three-inch heels because her attention was so riveted by the place. The small, subtle sign for Future, Inc. was barely visible from the road. Old maples and walnuts formed a canopy above the drive to the building, which was a sprawling redbrick with a couple of wings, a massive porch in front, landscaped grounds that wound around the place. It looked more like a gorgeous old home than a place of business—much less like a lab.

"My uncle's idea was for the place to fit in with the local historical look. Not to draw attention. A cold stone-and-glass type of building tends to make people think that the people and business are cold and stone-like, instead of caring. That was his theory, anyway. Of course, once you step inside…"

From the front door on, it was all high-tech. They could barely walk through a hallway before Harm had to identify himself with a key code, then a fingerprint code, and security alarm buttons were visible in every hall.

"We don't have any live guards," he said, "because the security system is so tight. Or we thought it was tight until the formula disappeared. Still, it's almost impossible for an outsider to get into. You'll see."

She did see. The first wing didn't hold just one lab, but a half dozen of them, each requiring a different set of security key codes. To Cate, the rooms looked something like ultra-contemporary kitchens, with stainless-steel tables and work counters and sinks—except for all the strange-looking equipment that she had no way to identify. The floors were spotless, and the air actually smelled fresh, with no hint of chemical or solvent that she could detect.

The last lab, at the end of one wing, had Yale and Purdue's name on the door, and required both handprint and eye identification to enter. It was the only lab that Harm opened, specifically so she could see how it fit into their ongoing crisis. "This is where the formula disappeared from." He motioned to a vault at the far end of the lab. "The computer work for it was on those two systems." He motioned again. "Of course, the factual data was also backed up on Fiske's system, and on mine. So whoever made it disappear had to sabotage everyone's private codes."

"Not something a dummy could pull off," she murmured.

"But knowing that hasn't helped. Everybody who works here has an IQ off the charts. It's easy to protect anything from an average thief—or even an extraordinary thief. But not from someone brilliant enough to create something brilliant to start with." He switched off the light and close-locked that door. "There's no reason for us to be in that lab, though, Cate. There's no point. It's already been gone over by security and cops and anyone who knows anything about the work. There is nothing there. Not related to the formula, not related to identifying who the culprit is. I'm positive."

"Okay." She trailed after him, feeling a building anxiety, not because of his lost formula, but because Harm's face was increasingly looking gray. He didn't yawn—God forbid he loosen up any of that army-general posture—but he was clearly stumbling tired.

The labs were all in the long west wing. The central wing held primarily community rooms. The break room had a semikitchen set up, with microwave and refrigerator…beyond that, Harm opened doors to reveal a couple of meeting rooms. Each had long tables, oversize chairs, windows overlooking the landscaping. "We call those the 'think tanks,'" he said, and then opened the last door in the central wing.

She shook her head. "What, you're running a motel on the side back here?"

He chuckled. "I know. It kind of looks that way." There were beds with different comforters, a huge flat-screen TV, couches. Unlike the pristine labs, this place looked mighty lived-in. Cate spotted a single shoe half under a bed, shirts and lab coats draped haphazardly on a coat tree, items strewn around—hairbrushes, open books, magazines, change, a belt.

"Explain," she said.

"Sometimes an experiment or trial has to be watched around the clock, and then one or more of the staff'll sleep over. Arthur always brought his dog, or so my uncle used to say."

Still, there was more. Harm showed her the supply rooms, where the side staff and apprentices worked, a massive general computer room. "So where's your lair?" she asked finally.

The far wing just held offices—Harm's, Fiske's and Arthur's.

His cell phone rang—which gave her a prize opportunity to nose around Harm's office without interference. This whole wing was carpeted in a thick, quiet blue, so with a mighty sigh of relief, she slipped off her shoes and kicked them out of the way. Immediately, she felt more like herself.

Harm's office was obviously originally his uncle's, and revealed a great deal about Dougal. Harm hadn't had time, or maybe the inclination, to clean out all his uncle's things. On the chestnut bookcases, Cate studied rows of framed photographs—many clearly of the wife Dougal had lost. Some shots were older, sixties by the look of the short skirts and hairstyles. There was a wedding picture, lots of flowers, a silky veil. In another, the two were riding horses. In another, they were hang gliding. In another, the pair wore climbing gear, both of them sweating and smiling.

It was obvious to Cate that the couple had not just loved each other, but loved doing things together, and were devoted to each other. The photos revealed the kind of love a woman dreamed of. The way his uncle loved, she mused, Harm would love, too…and savored the shots she found of him. Dougal had a terrific collection for her to pry into. Graduating pictures, vacation and holiday shots, some kind of science prize thing they'd done together. There was one shot of Harm with a woman— Cate pounced on it, studied it hard. The second wife, she thought. A beautiful woman, golden-skinned, almond eyes, satin black hair. Harm stood behind her, stiff, protectively. He was smiling…but he wasn't touching his bride.

Momentarily, the picture saddened her. Harm was such a toucher, such a man who came alive when he was touched. The picture told her all she wanted to know and more, about what he'd yet to have in his life. He may have loved—or even still love—his second wife.

But not like a man needed to love.

Not like Harm needed to be loved.

By the time he showed up back in the doorway, she'd touched and poked and opened and pried just about everywhere. The office had heaps of books, nests of papers. The desk chair was so old it should have been thrown out—but it was one of those kick-back, roll around, relax-in chairs. It was totally clear where and when Harm had taken over, because the credenza behind the desk was a total contrast—military-tidy, computer equipment lined up and spotless, files standing like soldiers.

"Hey, short stuff. You lost your shoes."

"They weren't shoes. They were torture devices."

She padded over, lifted up and kissed him. "Who was on the phone?"

"Just more information coming in. Still nothing that helps." He scraped a tired hand through his hair. "All three men, still no surprises. No hidden expenses, no hidden vices, no hidden bank accounts. Arthur apparently cheated on his wife twice, not once. Both times more than twenty years ago. And looking into people's lives like this…it makes me feel ugly down deep. I don't like intruding on their privacy. Finding out things that are none of my business."

She nodded. "But Harm…you weren't prying into their lives to intrude. You were trying to find information that would help you pin down the thief."

"I know. I'm just so damned frustrated…." Around then, he laid out a plan of attack. He wanted her to start digging in Fiske's office, and started unlocking doors and drawers, enabling her to access any and everything in Fiske's work space. "I know you're worried about the science, but like I keep telling you, don't be. We've had pros go into the science from every angle and found nothing. So all I want you to do is look around. Look for something that seems strange, something that jolts you when you look at it, something that doesn't belong."

"And you're going to be…?"

"Trying to do the same thing. In Arthur's office. And In Yale and Purdue's work areas." He glanced at her. "Cate, I know you don't believe this can matter, but I've come to believe—this might be the only way to find an answer. Experts have gone over the place from stem to stern and found nothing that's helped us. I really believe that your perceptions could bring something new to the problem."

It sounded like grasping at straws to Cate, but heaven knew, she'd do anything to come through for him. Fiske's office looked just like the man—homey, comfortable and capable, generally tidy.

She parked herself in front of Fiske's computer first, because once Harm had given her passwords and security keys, she knew how to roam around that kind of technology. Two hours passed before she realized it. Startled at how easily she'd become engrossed, she wandered around to stretch her legs, find a bathroom, then hit the break room to make coffee and see if she could scare up some snacks.

She tracked down Harm, weaving on his feet in front of a stand-up computer in a security vault. About to offer him something to eat, she changed her mind. "Okay," she said, "that's it. You're taking a nap."

"No."

"Do you ever want to have sex with me again?"

His eyes narrowed. "You'd do that? Bargain with sex? I thought you were a better woman than that."

"Well, you're wrong. I'm absolutely no better. I saw the couch in your office." She put one hand on her hip and motioned with a royal finger toward his office.

"I'm not—"

"We're both locked in this place. Couldn't be safer in church. All life will not end if you take two or three hours for a short crash. Now go."

"I won't sleep. Can't sleep."

"Fine. Prove it. I'll check on you in ten minutes. If

you're not asleep by then, I promise I'll let you back at it."

He considered this. "You have a really ugly side to you, Cate. Manipulative. Controlling. Dictatorial."

"You know perfectly well that compliments go straight to my head, so don't waste your breath. Go."

She checked on him ten minutes later, and found him sleeping so deeply she wasn't sure she could have roused him with a cattle prod. Mentally, she debated whether to scare up a blanket from the sleepover room, but it didn't seem that cold, so she just tucked his jacket over him, switched off the glaring overhead light and left him to rest.

Instead of steering straight back to Fiske's office, she detoured to the break room, brewed a fresh pot of coffee and prowled around the cupboards for something to snack on—then realized she couldn't be less hungry. An odd shiver chased up her spine. Even though she wanted Harm to catch some sleep, suddenly she felt spooked by the realization that she was completely alone in the building.

Which, of course, was stupid. She was perfectly happy doing anything alone. She'd never been afraid of being alone.

Back in Fiske's office, she turned on the spare lamps as well as the overhead, pulled up the chair ottoman, and started going through every single thing in every single drawer and file.

His computer, at least, had held interesting stuff, such as e-mails with other scientists, old university colleagues, cancer research sites around the world.

The stuff in his files was just financial. Boring, endless numbers. Nothing that meant anything to her.

She caught herself yawning, figured lack of sleep was catching up with her, too—it was almost five in the morning by then.

And then she hit pay dirt.

She thought.

She pushed aside the ottoman and plunked down on the carpet to spread out a fan of papers. Maybe she was nuts, but sometimes it seemed as if Fiske totally changed his handwriting style. When she pulled out the examples of this, she had notes and calendar entries and files or reports with memos scratched on the side.

By themselves, they didn't seem to mean much. The scratched handwriting said things like "Ask Yale and Purdue." Or "See Arthur." One note had a figure, $89,945, underlined with question marks. There was another handwritten memo to check on records from November and February from the year before…and another legal sheet of paper with a series of numbers, handwritten, rather than produced from a computer report or printer. She wasn't positive of the exact day that Dougal had died, but from the timetable Harm had given her, Fiske must have been accumulating those numbers from that same week.

She hunched over, and started pulling every scrap of paper together that illustrated the odd change in handwriting, trying to analyze why it had drawn her attention.

It was about emotion, she thought, and figured any normal person would laugh at her for drawing such an unprovable conclusion. Maybe Harm would laugh, too—but he'd listen to her. He'd listened to her about the peppermint. So far, he'd listened to her whenever she said anything.

Could you fall in love with a man, just for that?

Stick to the problem, she yelled at herself, and promptly knocked over her coffee—not a major problem, because there were only a few cold drops left in the cup.

She didn't know what any of the numbers or dates meant, but everything else that Fiske had written by hand had shown neat, tidy letters, a clear script. The sudden ink-heavy notes and splash of letters was different, as if Fiske were upset or concerned.

She wasn't sure how to pull all the scraps together—by date, chronological order? By notes versus numbers? By names? By…

Abruptly she heard a sound, and looked up with her heart pounding. There was nothing there. Obviously. But for a second she felt so unnerved that she bounced to her feet and scurried down the long hall to Harm's office.

He hadn't moved, even an inch. He was still sleeping so deeply that she just couldn't imagine waking him. What difference could another hour make? Besides, she had more to go through…and another hour would give her a chance to organize it all somehow.

Unfortunately, she was lagging hard now, too. Her eyes were stinging dry, the back of her neck tight and achy. She hit the restroom to splash cold water on her face, then refilled her mug with coffee, hoping the caffeine would give her a second wind. She carted the steaming mug back to Fiske's office, zoomed in the door…and dropped the mug, splashing hot coffee all over herself and the rug and papers.

Purdue hadn't made a sound. He was standing absolutely quietly, behind the door.

He closed the door, just as quietly, before she'd even had the chance to open her mouth in a scream.

Chapter 12

"Well, darn, Cate." Purdue sounded as easy and amiable as an old friend who'd just stopped by. "I hope you didn't burn yourself."

"You scared the wits out of me!" Instinctively, Cate bent down, brushing at where the hot coffee had splashed on her bare legs. But she barely felt the burning liquid. If anything, she felt suddenly cold from the inside out.

Acid cold.

Sour cold.

So cold she could taste it in the very back of her throat.

"I didn't mean to scare you." Purdue took another step toward her. "I didn't expect anyone to be in the building. There was no other car parked in front. Nothing but the usual security lights on that I could see when I first came in."

"I'm parked in back." Of all the insane things to talk about. She pushed at a coffee spot on her black dinner dress—as if that wasn't an insane thing to worry about, too. Cripes, he was probably going to kill her. Who cared if she had a dry-cleaning bill? It was just... Purdue didn't seem any more dangerous now than he had before.

He looked tired, of course. Travel tired. But he was wearing a crisp-enough white button-down shirt over jeans, labeled sandals; his hair was neatly brushed, his thin black glasses adding to his look of Ivy-League cool. His smile still had charm. His confidence still glowed.

He was still annoying.

He let out another quiet bark of a laugh. "I just can't get over it. Of all the people I might have expected to find here, much less at five in the morning, it never crossed my mind that you might be one of them."

"That certainly goes both ways. I thought you and Yale were on the same flight, not getting in for hours yet."

"Yeah, that was the last plan...but I was willing to upgrade to first-class, just to get home sooner."

"And after all that traveling, you came right to work, even in the middle of the night."

He nodded. She figured out why she felt so cold now. His eyes, his gaze, centered on every movement she made, every expression on her face. But behind those black-framed glasses, his eyes seemed as blank as black ice. Of course, she might be cold for another reason.

Like being scared out of her wits.

"Naturally, I came here. I suspect the rest will show up as soon as they can conceivably get here. We're all concerned about finding answers to our little lab mystery. Why don't you sit down, Cate? You look as if you're about to fall down anyway."

Aw, hell. She was a lousy pretender, and sooner or later she was going to put her foot in her mouth, anyway, so might as well get it all over with. "You're not here to look for answers," she said. "You don't need to do that. You already know the whole story—because it's your story, isn't it? You're the one."

He didn't bother responding, just motioned to the mess of papers on the carpet in front of Fiske's desk. "I take it that you're the one who's been putting all this stuff together."

"Yes." She wasn't sure if he realized Harm was in the building. Surely, he couldn't believe Harm would leave her here alone in the middle of the night? But…she'd turned off the light in Harm's office. If Purdue had just been looking around, he wouldn't have seen any other sign of life but her. In the one office he was the most interested in: Fiske's.

"Well, you probably think you know a whole lot, then, don't you? But you'd be wrong. It's not what it looks like, Cate. I didn't steal a damn thing."

"Right. That's why you're here before daybreak. Because you were just trying to be helpful for the team."

He met her eyes. "Look at me. Look at my face. I did not steal anything. That's the truth."

Silently, she studied him. Clearly, she was never going

to make it as a judge because he looked as sincere as an innocent kid. He was a pain, yes, but as far as she could tell, he wasn't lying. Still, even believing him, her stomach was suddenly twisting and her heart thumping a wild, petrified drumbeat. "All right," she said.

"All those papers on the floor—I didn't have time to really look at what you've been putting together there. But it doesn't matter. No one will ever find proof that I stole anything. Because I didn't."

That sure sounded as if he were protesting too much, Cate thought, but she could hardly credit that judgment. Just then, she wasn't sure she had enough judgment to wad a BB gun. The fluorescent overheads reflected on Purdue's face, gave his skin a plaster cast. One second, her heart was screaming, *Harm, for God's sake, wake up and find me!* and in the next second, she was scared witless that Purdue would quit talking—and definitely quit playing nice—if he knew Harm was here, so she didn't want Harm awake at all.

So that was the thing. She couldn't think. Couldn't stop feeling creeped out. Couldn't stop feeling keening sad that she'd never told Harm she loved him, and darn it, that she owed her sisters e-mails, and unless something brilliant happened—something she hadn't thought of yet—she could well be dead before this was over and Purdue gotten away scot-free with even more than he already had.

"How did you get in?" she asked. "I thought this place was wired so secure that nothing and no one could get in."

"It is. But I'm one of the few who have to get into the

lab at all hours of the day and night. Naturally, Harm changed all the codes and security arrangements after the so-called theft. But it wasn't hard to break into the new system. Harm…he's got that military background, but overall, he just can't seem to help thinking like an honest man."

"Yeah, that's a big fault of his," Cate readily agreed.

"Where I have a scientist's mind. I love puzzles. I love logic. Figuring out the new codes was no tougher than the *New York Times* Sunday crossword. Move aside, Cate."

He didn't have a gun—or any other weapon—in sight. But when he crouched down, his gaze darted from the papers she'd spread out to her face. Whatever he saw in those quick glances to the records she'd put together never changed the expression on his face. But he reached in his pocket and pulled out a book of matches.

She only had one button that couldn't be pushed, that she had no defense for. And he just found it. "Wait," she said.

"Just step back. How about if you sit in Fiske's chair behind that big old comfortable desk. Relax. Nothing terrible is going to happen." He straightened up, keeping his eyes on her face, and moved a few steps to locate the wastebasket under the desk. He dumped out its contents, then carried the basket to the center of the floor. "Cate. You've got a real skittery look in your eyes. Chill. You don't want to make me do something we'd both regret. Nothing bad has to happen. To you, to me, to anyone."

The wastebasket wasn't a standard issue metal basket

like offices usually had, but was leather, with gold-embossing. A gift someone had given Fiske, she thought. Which was very nice, except that the surface was a ton more flammable than a metal container. "There are a bunch more papers," she said desperately.

Purdue, about to bend down to stuff papers in the basket, abruptly shot his head up. "Where?"

"All over."

He made a sound of disbelief. "Yeah. Right. But just for the record, I really would like to know how you came across all this stuff. Where was it? It's not as if I hadn't looked before. Hell. We all looked. Lawyers looked. Cops looked. Everyone looked."

But Cate suspected they'd all been looking for some kind of direct evidence to the cancer formula. She wouldn't have been able to identify that if her life depended on it. All she'd been able to notice was the change in Fiske's handwriting—the slant, the pressure of ink—that indicated Fiske was upset about something.

But she didn't waste time telling Purdue that, because she couldn't imagine he'd believe her. Until she saw his reaction to her collection of notes and papers, she hadn't been all that positive she had anything that important besides.

"Purdue," she said, "there are more records and papers all over, in different files and drawers and computer records. I'd just started looking and come up with this much." She added quickly, "I could help you look for more."

His hands shook, but it didn't stop him from heaping all the records she'd collected into the leather wastebasket. Then he patted his pocket, looking for the book of matches again. His good-looking features seemed waxier by the minute. She couldn't see madness or meanness in his face, but for certain there was exhaustion. Bone-deep exhaustion. End-of-his-rope exhaustion.

He was so tired she wasn't sure what he'd do...or what he was capable of.

"Listen," she said urgently, "I don't know what happened. I don't know why you did whatever you did. But I'm sure you had a good reason. If you explained to Harm what happened—"

"I didn't steal *anything!* I told you that!"

"Okay, okay, take it easy." She tried to remember how to breathe normally. "Tell me. How I can help you?"

Wrong question. Wrong, wrong, wrong question. She was used to saying the wrong thing at the wrong time, but sheesh. His jaw tightened as if it had suddenly been wired.

"You want to help me? You could have helped me by not being in this office. By not finding any of these records. By not being in the middle of this. I *never* wanted to hurt you. I never wanted to hurt Fiske. I never wanted to hurt Dougal. It just got out of control. One mistake, and everywhere I turned, it multiplied. It got so messed up I didn't know what to do, how to make it right again. How to make *anything* right again."

"Tell me," she said, and took a tiptoe-quiet step back toward the door. Something about his face, his expression, had changed. She was gut-scared now. Soul-scared. Any options she thought she had, Cate now figured were out the window. She only had one. To get out of there.

"My mother...I couldn't do anything wrong in her eyes. But my dad was a real different story. Growing up, I couldn't please him to save my life. Beat the hell out of me, any excuse he could think of. Only then I got a full scholarship to Purdue, and it all changed. It wasn't just that I'd grown up, got too big to hit. It was more like...I'd gone to a place where he didn't want to hurt me anymore. He got off on telling neighbors and friends that I was brilliant. Perfect. Turned into the ideal son. Doing something. Only I couldn't live up to it. Who can be perfect all the time? It's not like I went looking to screw up. It just happened. It was wrong, but it was just a stupid mistake. It just...it got out of hand so fast. Yale, he was right next to me, he didn't know what was going on. He hasn't got a brain. You'd think coming from Yale, he'd be the smart one, wouldn't you?"

He seemed to expect her to agree with him, so she carefully nodded. "You'd think," she echoed.

"Yeah. But he wasn't. *I* was the smart one. And that was the thing. It could all have disappeared. No one would have figured it out. The formula really was gone, and it was going to be a mystery that no one could ever solve."

"Purdue—please, please don't do that—" She saw that he'd found the matchbook again, had flipped it open to snap off a match. "Don't set a fire. Please."

She didn't tell him that her parents had died in a fire, that visions of those flames, her mom's cries, her dad silhouetted in the dark window were in all her nightmares. She never told anyone, and she'd certainly never reveal such a vulnerable thing to him. But…she couldn't breathe, looking at the book of matches.

Purdue glanced at her, diverted by her tone, but only for a couple seconds. "No reason to get your liver in an uproar. All I'm doing is burning these papers. They don't prove anything. They just look like they prove something. They look like someone's guilty of something."

"And you're not guilty," she said, trying to appease him, to calm him.

"I'm not guilty of stealing. Just of making a mistake. That's all it started out to be, a stupid mistake. I wish the old man, Dougal, hadn't figured it out. But after that, I didn't think anyone would get it. I could quit worrying. I was going to be right here, doing my job, nothing different for me. You're right, though, Cate."

"Right?"

"After I burn this round, I'll keep looking for more papers. How far'd you get?"

"I don't know." Her eyes seemed to be burned open on that matchbook, the match, his shaking fingers.

"Well, whatever else there could be still has to be in Fiske's office. He was the only other one who figured it out. He cornered me on the boat. He still didn't actually know what he'd found, but he knew it was wrong, knew some things hadn't added up, knew it was about me. I wasn't thinking about the peppermint, until you made those cookies. I saw how he loved 'em. It was a dentist who told me about this guy, how he'd burned up his throat just trying to make a toothache go away, took too much, didn't know. I never wanted to hurt Fiske. I loved him, we all did. I didn't want to hurt anyone, I swear—"

"Purdue, *please*. Please don't—"

He ignored her. Cate wasn't positive he was even talking to her by then; he seemed to be muttering to himself. And she was only half listening, because she couldn't hear him. All her concentration focused on him striking the match. It was an old restaurant book of matches. The first one didn't spark.

He pulled another match from the book, tried again.

She saw the tiny flame…and flew. Flew at the flame, flew at him. She crashed a knee at the corner of the desk, saw the startled surprise in Purdue's eyes, kept going.

The match flamed out, dropped, somewhere in the seconds when she dived on top of Purdue. They both tangled to the floor.

"Harm!" she screamed, but could barely get his name from her throat before Purdue reacted. He grabbed a fistful of her hair, tugged, wrenching every hair root on her head.

"Harm!" she screamed again.

Harm woke up with a jolt, for a moment disoriented by the dim room and crunchy leather couch beneath him. In an instant, of course, he recognized his office at the lab, and swung to his feet.

He could only think of one conceivable reason why he could possibly feel rested…

Cate had let him sleep.

Alarm hustled his heartbeat. She'd never really gotten it, that danger wasn't like on TV where the bad guys always behaved in identifiable ways. Even good people could do unforgivable things if they were pushed to the wall. He'd known that forever. Just couldn't nail which of the men had been pushed past the breaking point, no matter how hard he'd tried, and damn, but there was too little time left.

Rolling his shoulders to chase out some stiff kinks, he aimed first for the restroom and second for the coffee machine.

Five-ten, his watch claimed. She'd let him sleep for hours.

He figured he'd pour two fresh cups, one for her— even though he was going to yell at her when he delivered it.

And that was when he heard her muffled scream.

Both mugs clattered to the floor. He turned the corner at turbo speed, saw the door to Fiske's office was closed, added up the bad news on instinct.

He backtracked, hit the security button just inside Arthur's office—because it was the closest one—then sprinted toward Fiske's. All the doors automatically locked when they were closed—yet another security measure he'd put in—but now it took him blasted, insanely long seconds to jab in the key code. He knew it, knew every key code in the whole damned place, but his usually terrific memory jammed up. Finally, finally, he heard the final click, then yanked at the doorknob.

He didn't stop moving, didn't have to, saw Cate's body twisted half on, half under Purdue's, and leaped in.

His hands clawed at Purdue's shoulders, startling him, offering Harm a second's advantage. It was all he needed. He yanked Purdue off, slammed him against the desk.

Cate yelped, scuttled out of the way, but it wasn't over.

Something in Purdue sensed that he had nothing left to lose. Harm could see it in his eyes. He was desperate and cornered, and when he launched himself back at Harm, he went straight for the throat.

Harm twisted, went for a knee shot, but Purdue only gripped tighter, squeezed harder. Harm punched his weight into a roll, battered him back against the desk in a shattering head-knock, but Purdue still clawed tight around his neck. Harm saw red, then white, couldn't find any air anywhere, anyhow.

But giving up wasn't a choice. Giving up would have left Cate alone with a madman. That couldn't happen. Wouldn't happen. He twisted, stabbed, kicked. One of the kicks finally connected, because he heard Purdue gasp and loosen that nail-tight grip on his neck, just a little—but it was enough.

Harm jerked back, gasping for air and aiming a punch at the same time…only to see a picture frame crack on Purdue's head. Glass shattered in a shower of tiny splinters. Purdue fell back, blood streaming from the gash on the side of his head.

Harm sank back, momentarily wrung out as much from relief as needing a minute to let his body recover.

He wanted to laugh at the sight of Cate still bending over Purdue with the broken picture frame in her hands…but humor was really the last thing on his mind.

He met her eyes…and slowly lifted a hand.

She met his eyes…and slowly lowered a hand.

Their fingertips touched. Just the tips. The most basic communication that it was over, they'd both survived it, they were together. In that instant, in that crazily tender connection, Harm found a soul mate like he'd never imagined.

Then came the smiles. "Are you all right?"

Her hands were shaking. Her new black dinner dress had a sharp rip. A bruise was already coloring on her cheek and upper arm. But she answered the real question that mattered. "Fine. Ready to party," Cate said. "You?"

"Couldn't be better." His throat felt raw-burned. His still couldn't work up any volume in his voice, was starting to feel swelling in a knee and right hand. "Although I seem to be hearing sirens."

The place was flooded with people by daybreak. Three carloads of police had showed up, along with an ambulance. Harm suspected that any high-level crime must be mighty rare in Cambridge, because everyone and his mother arrived to help, even if it was barely dawn on a Sunday morning.

Cate was separated from him for a while. He wasn't sure who took her off or to where. The two ambulance medics seemed to think he needed some first aid—and for damn sure, Purdue did. The lead cop was a woman.

She identified herself as Smythe, had some experienced life lines on her face, and came across as a one-woman army—efficient, cool, unshakeable. She pulled up a chair between him and Purdue.

"Something tells me this is too complicated to get any quick answers to," she said.

"You've got that right. The bottom line is that Purdue—whose real name is John Henry Swisher—" Harm motioned to Purdue, who'd barely moved since the medic bent over him "—is a murderer, thief and embezzler. Although it'll take a while to get it all laid out in black and white."

For the first time, Purdue spoke. "Connolly. Harm. I need to talk you—alone."

"You think? If I ever get you alone, you turkey, your face will never be that pretty again. You hurt Cate."

"She jumped me. She was on top of me. She hit me with the picture frame. I didn't do anything to her—"

"You pushed her off the top deck in Alaska. Did you forget that?"

The medic finished swabbing the side of Purdue's face with something purple and started applying gauze. Purdue started to deny the accusation and swallowed instead.

Harm, never long on patience, jumped him—or almost did. The cool-eyed lieutenant's face carefully got in his way. "I can do far more damage than you can," Smythe promised him.

"You could also leave the room for just a couple of minutes."

But Purdue wanted to keep talking. "Harm,

whatever you think, at least let me set part of the record straight."

Harm figured he was just going to hear excuses. He didn't want to hear them. He was still seeing sick-red from mental instant replay of Cate struggling with the jerk, her eyes drenched with fear, her face pale with it. He didn't doubt she'd jumped Purdue. He didn't doubt she'd jump a bear—or a whale. Damn woman had more courage than an army.

But she wasn't used to dealing with criminals.

Hell, none of them were.

"There never *was* a formula, Harm. That's the thing. The cure for pancreatic cancer—we never had it. We were close. We're *still* close. Your uncle was so positive that we'd turned a corner, finally found the right track. Yale and I were here, night after night, doing trials…"

"Just spill it out," Harm gruffed. All right, he couldn't help but listen. And the lieutenant was certainly engaged. But since nothing was being recorded, nothing really counted—at least not in a court of law, where it mattered. So all Harm really wanted out of life right then was Cate. He wanted her in sight. Within touching range. Immediately. Nonstop for the next thirty years, give or take an extra thirty.

Still, Purdue was willing to confess. And for the sake of his uncle and everyone else involved in the lab, Harm really did want to find out whatever happened that turned this extraordinarily wonderful place into a nightmare.

"One of those nights, I was exhausted, really wiped, so I took a little something to stay awake," Purdue

admitted. The medic finished with the bandaging and
started packing up the first-aid gear.

"You mean some kind of amphetamine?"

"Don't tell me you never did anything in college,"
Purdue defended.

"I never did anything in college," Harm said. "Just
go on with the damned story."

"The thing was…I must have dropped some. I did
drop some. Into the formula we were working on."

Harm frowned, listening hard now. "How much?
What exactly was it?"

"I don't know."

"The hell you don't."

"No. This is the thing. I fell asleep. The next thing I
knew, it was morning, and Yale had just gotten to work,
so had your uncle…and they were shaking me, waking
me up, all excited, because the trial I was finishing up
the night before had *worked*. Really worked. The results
were everything we'd ever dreamed of. Only…I didn't
realize about the accidental addition into the formula
until I got home, looked for my bottle, and there was
nothing in it. The top was even gone, so I knew it had
spilled."

"Are you talking one pill, two, what?"

"It was a mix of different things. Several different
things. I drove back to the lab immediately that same
night. I looked everywhere. You know how things were
locked up in that back lab. No one had been in there, not
cleaning staff or anyone else. So if I could have found
the pills…but I didn't…because there was nothing to

find. They'd become part of the formula. No one knew that but me, and I obviously couldn't tell anyone."

The lieutenant had clearly made a choice to stay silent, to let Purdue confess all he was willing to without distractions, but now she interjected. "What exactly are you talking about here? One specific amphetamine? Or a mix with cocaine or E or—?"

"It was a cocktail. A mix of different things. I'd gotten it before, from a friend I knew. A friend who'd given it to me before."

"But you don't know exactly what was in this cocktail?"

"No. I was exhausted that night. And after that…I just didn't know what to do. It all just…exploded. Everybody was so happy with the success. Everybody believed we got the dream, a cure for one of the worst cancers there is. Everybody thinking we were all going to be rich. But because of it all, Dougal suddenly tripled the security on everything. Nobody worked alone on anything after that, even for short periods of time. The idea was to protect us all, make sure we were watching out for each other, not because he didn't trust us to work alone. But by then, Dougal, he wanted everything exactly right, verifiably right, so there were two people on every procedure we did…."

Purdue raised stricken eyes to Harm. A boy's lost eyes. "The work I did here…it was the best thing that ever happened to me. My father…growing up, he was meaner than a snake to me, to my mother. That never changed until I got into college. It's not like I was still afraid of him after that. It was more like…I could taste the revenge. No one in the family had gone this far, certainly not him. He started telling everybody how good I was, how important—"

Harm shook his head impatiently. "That story would have worked on me—and I know my uncle would have listened. If you'd just come clean when this happened."

"But I'm telling you why I couldn't. No one *knew*. I was the only one, and it was just a *mistake*. I never intentionally did anything wrong to the work. In fact, I was part of the reason we'd gotten so far—"

"Only then my uncle died." Harm knew the next sequence in the story.

"I had to get to that formula. I had to make it disappear. That's all I wanted to do. I never wanted to hurt anyone. I just wanted it to disappear before someone discovered that the formula on paper would never work again. It wasn't really stealing, Harm. I didn't gain from it. I was just trying to make my mistake go away."

Harm figured Purdue'd be happy to spew out more excuses until the cows came home. He interrupted with something that had preyed on his mind for weeks. "You killed my uncle."

"No. No. That was accidental. Completely accidental. We were alone in the lab, early one morning. He was so happy. This was what he dreamed of, the only thing in life he really wanted, not for the money, but the cure. But he couldn't understand why we'd been unable to duplicate the one perfect batch, you know? So that's why we were in there so early...."

"And?"

"And…I thought I could tell him. At that point, I knew I had to tell him. He was suspecting that something was wrong. He was going to figure it out—he'd been involved in the trials and experiments for more years than any of us. He could see something was off, was analyzing, trying to pin it down…so I told him because I had to. I thought maybe even he'd understand. Only then…"

"You killed him."

"I didn't. He…just…fell to the ground. He started crying like a kid. Then he started holding his chest. He wasn't that old, you know? I swear I didn't actually realize he was having a heart attack—"

Harm listened for another ten minutes. But then he'd heard all he could take.

Chapter 13

Cate had to open half the cupboards in the break room to find anything remotely edible. Finally, she came across some paper plates. Doritos. A few slices of leftover cheese and things in the fridge.

She shook out the Doritos, unsure whether she was feeling more mad or hurt. Actually, there was no real contest. Anger won the prize.

For sure, she had some hurts—a variety of bruises from the ugly tangle with Purdue. Her head was pounding from a lack-of-sleep headache. She'd ruined her new black dinner dress. She'd had the hiccups twice in the last hour, and every time she thought of that tussle with Purdue, she got another case.

It wasn't every day she ran into a criminal. It had been a story until today. A TV script. Fiske had died and she'd been pushed off the deck of the boat and things had happened, but none of it had been real until Purdue had his hands on her today. She'd never been afraid of anything in her life before, and now, when she really needed to curl up in someone's arms and feel safe for a while—the stupid lab was filled with strangers. Why on earth so many police had shown up, she had no idea, but they'd obviously shown up to help, and it was a ghastly hour on a Sunday morning, and none of them could have had time for any kind of food. There was no breakfast food to be had in the entire place. She'd brewed fresh coffee and then tea, but that wasn't food.

On top of which, Harm had been closeted in Fiske's office with Purdue and the lieutenant and medics—and everybody else, practically, but her.

Like she was invisible.

Like she hadn't been through hell and a half herself.

Sniffing—loudly—she used the worst paring knife she'd ever seen to create slivers of cheese, sprinkled them on the Doritos, found some dried onions...what a disgrace!...and then popped the plate in the microwave for a few seconds. Possibly she slammed the door on the microwave, but she figured she was entitled.

Her feet hurt, too.

She'd almost forgotten that.

When the microwave pinged, all of thirty seconds later, she reached for the door—and saw Harm. Standing right there in the doorway. As if he'd been watching her forever! When she'd needed him! And she'd been miserable!

Only then she saw the expression on his face.

She didn't lose all that being mad. She just flew across the room and threw her arms around him. "Hey. Everything's all right. You're safe, I'm safe. It's going to be all right."

He clung and clung and clung. Or maybe she was the one doing some of that heavy-duty clinging, but darn it, he looked terrible—all rumpled, his cheek swelling up, his shirt ripped, a cut above his eyebrow he'd gotten heaven-knew-how, whiskers on his chin. The worst, though, the really worst, were his eyes. She'd never seen him look so...sad...before. It was unbearable.

"There was no formula, Cate."

"No?"

"They were working on a real-enough formula. But the one they thought successful—hell, I don't know if it actually was, but it almost doesn't matter, because it can't be duplicated. So. We don't have our cure."

She couldn't make total sense of what he said, but she got the picture. Purdue had faked the formula somehow, and that was the catalyst that switched on the rest of the nightmare. Eventually, she'd ask him about all the hows and whys.

Right then, she was absorbed in what he didn't say— the part that really hurt. Harm didn't give a damn about money, never would. He cared about saving the world. He was pretty much that kind of hopeless, cockamamie idealist.

"Hey," she said, real rough and tough. She leaned back, not wanting to sever that hug, but...well, there were a lot of people around. "All you're really saying is that we don't have our cure now, Harm. You've got years and years to work with this. Starting exactly where your uncle left off, and that was darned close to success, right?"

When she broke free from him, he said immediately, "Wherever you think you're going, come back here."

"Believe me, I'm going right back in your arms, buster. But I promised the boys something…." She took the plate from the microwave. "It's pretty disgusting, I know, especially for breakfast. But there was just nothing around here for me to work with, so…"

She sprinted out of the room, and sprinted right back in about three seconds later with empty hands. "I just felt bad that so many of them came, that they all had to get up so early. Nobody had time for breakfast, and then they were stuck, just hanging and waiting while you were in there with the lieutenant and Purdue."

"You are such a caretaker." He leaned back against the counter and shook his head.

She bristled. "I most certainly am not!"

"You are. You take care of everyone. You sure as hell have taken outstanding care of me." He started walking toward her, one slow step at a time.

She put her hands on her hips. "Just because I'm a chef doesn't mean I fit the stereotype of the waiting-on-a-man kind of woman. That kind of caretaking role went out in the Middle Ages, you know."

"I realize you can't help it. I suspect it's hardwired in your DNA. So we're not going to talk about how many babies we're going to have."

Her hand slapped her chest, as if that might help keep her heart from imploding. "Harm, neither of us has had a good night's sleep in ages," she said reasonably. "We've both been battered and beat-up tonight. And terrified. We've only known each other for a very, very, very short time…."

She would have gone on, but he interrupted.

"You're in love with me. And I know damn well I'm in love with you—the way I've never been in love, the way I've never loved anyone else. Now Cate, I realize you have commitment issues…"

"I don't have issues! I'm against commitment altogether!"

He nodded. "I know. But Cookie, I'm not leaving you. I'm not going to die in a fire. I plan on hanging around in your life until we're both white-haired and crotchety—not that you're not already crotchety. I don't want to insult you by implying that your heart's bigger than the sky, and that you're the warmest, most giving woman I've ever known. I do love you, Cate."

"Stop it. You're making me nervous!"

His mouth crooked up in a grin. "Good. I'll practice doing that every day. And in the meantime…I just don't think you're the kind of woman who can sit around, rolling in money every day with nothing to do…"

She wasn't about to let that slur to her character slip by. "Hey, I could do that. I'm lazy. And greedy."

"Uh-huh." From his tone, he was obviously ignoring her. "So I've been thinking. This is my theory. You open a restaurant here."

The idea lodged in her mind like a thorn. A sweet thorn. She had no idea how much she wanted it, how

much she'd yearned to open her own place, until the
blasted man had said the idea aloud. "What?"

"I'll stake you. But I have terms."

"What terms?"

"You wear my ring. Left hand."

Since he seemed to be still walking toward her, she
lifted her arms. It was so easy...to just walk right into
the warmth of his embrace. "You've given out rings
before," she reminded him.

"Not like this. Cate. You're the one."

Damnation. A place full of police, no sleep, nerves
and heart frayed by everything wrong going on... But
when he kissed her right then, the world didn't stand
still. The way he kissed her, her whole world spun like
a star.

"Harm?"

"Tell me," he encouraged her.

"I love you. I'm in love with you. But I've been afraid
to tell you, to say it. I don't doubt how I feel. But...I've
never trusted in the future, Harm. I'm not sure that I
know how."

He nodded. "But that's exactly the thing, Cate. You
can tell me what you're afraid of. Then we can work
with it together. The way you've worked on this crisis
with me. Together. It's all right to be afraid."

"It isn't."

He whispered, "Yeah. It is. With me. I promise."
And he proved it, showing her with kiss after kiss after
kiss...

Eventually the ambulance left. And the police.
Finally, there was no one there but the two of them.

Sunlight streamed in the windows, a warm day heating up outside, the promise of a future whispering in the breeze. In his kisses. In her heart.

He was right. She could be vulnerable. With him.

* * * * *

Look for Cate's sister, Lily's story in
IRRESISTIBLE STRANGER, the next book
in Jennifer Greene's exciting
NEW MAN IN TOWN *miniseries.*

COMING NEXT MONTH

Available September 28, 2010

ROMANTIC SUSPENSE

SRSCNM0910

REQUEST YOUR FREE BOOKS!

2 FREE NOVELS
PLUS
2 FREE GIFTS!

Silhouette®

ROMANTIC
SUSPENSE

Sparked by Danger, Fueled by Passion.

YES! Please send me 2 FREE Silhouette® Romantic Suspense novels and my 2 FREE gifts (gifts are worth about $10). After receiving them, if I don't wish to receive any more books, I can return the shipping statement marked "cancel." If I don't cancel, I will receive 4 brand-new novels every month and be billed just $4.24 per book in the U.S. or $4.99 per book in Canada. That's a saving of 15% off the cover price! It's quite a bargain! Shipping and handling is just 50¢ per book.* I understand that accepting the 2 free books and gifts places me under no obligation to buy anything. I can always return a shipment and cancel at any time. Even if I never buy another book from Silhouette, the two free books and gifts are mine to keep forever.

240/340 SDN E5Q4

Name	(PLEASE PRINT)

Address	Apt. #

City	State/Prov.	Zip/Postal Code

Signature (if under 18, a parent or guardian must sign)

Mail to the Silhouette Reader Service:
IN U.S.A.: P.O. Box 1867, Buffalo, NY 14240-1867
IN CANADA: P.O. Box 609, Fort Erie, Ontario L2A 5X3

Not valid for current subscribers to Silhouette Romantic Suspense books.

Want to try two free books from another line?
Call 1-800-873-8635 or visit www.morefreebooks.com.

* Terms and prices subject to change without notice. Prices do not include applicable taxes. N.Y. residents add applicable sales tax. Canadian residents will be charged applicable provincial taxes and GST. Offer not valid in Quebec. This offer is limited to one order per household. All orders subject to approval. Credit or debit balances in a customer's account(s) may be offset by any other outstanding balance owed by or to the customer. Please allow 4 to 6 weeks for delivery. Offer available while quantities last.

Your Privacy: Silhouette is committed to protecting your privacy. Our Privacy Policy is available online at www.eHarlequin.com or upon request from the Reader Service. From time to time we make our lists of customers available to reputable third parties who may have a product or service of interest to you. If you would prefer we not share your name and address, please check here. ☐

Help us get it right—We strive for accurate, respectful and relevant communications. To clarify or modify your communication preferences, visit us at www.ReaderService.com/consumerchoice.

SRS10R

*See below for a sneak peek at
our inspirational line, Love Inspired®.
Introducing HIS HOLIDAY BRIDE
by bestselling author Jillian Hart*

Autumn Granger gave her horse rein to slide toward the town's new sheriff.

"Hey, there." The man in a brand-new Stetson, black T-shirt, jeans and riding boots held up a hand in greeting. He stepped away from his four-wheel drive with "Sheriff" in black on the doors and waded through the grasses. "I'm new around here."

"I'm Autumn Granger."

"Nice to meet you, Miss Granger. I'm Ford Sherman, from Chicago." He knuckled back his hat, revealing the most handsome face she'd ever seen. Big blue eyes contrasted with his sun-tanned complexion.

"I'm guessing you haven't seen much open land. Out here, you've got to keep an eye on cows or they're going to tear your vehicle apart."

"What?" He whipped around. Sure enough, mammoth black-and-white creatures had started to gnaw on his four-wheel drive. They clustered like a mob, mouths and tongues and teeth bent on destruction. One cow tried to pry the wiper off the windshield, another chewed on the side mirror. Several leaned through the open window, licking the seats.

"Move along, little dogie." He didn't know the first thing about cattle.

The entire herd swiveled their heads to study him curiously. Not a single hoof shifted. The animals soon returned to chewing, licking, digging through his possessions.

Autumn laughed, a warm and wonderful sound. "Thanks,

I needed that." She then pulled a bag from behind her saddle and waved it at the cows. "Look what I have, guys. Cookies."

Cows swung in her direction, and dozens of liquid brown eyes brightened with cookie hopes. As she circled the car, the cattle bounded after her. The earth shook with the force of their powerful hooves.

"Next time, you're on your own, city boy." She tipped her hat. The cowgirl stayed on his mind, the sweetest thing he had ever seen.

Will Ford be able to stick it out in the country
to find out more about Autumn?
Find out in HIS HOLIDAY BRIDE
by bestselling author Jillian Hart,
available in October 2010
only from Love Inspired®.

Copyright © 2010 by Jill Strickler

SHLIEXP1010

FROM #1 *NEW YORK TIMES*
AND *USA TODAY* BESTSELLING AUTHOR

DEBBIE MACOMBER

Mrs. Miracle on 34th Street...

This Christmas, Emily Merkle (just call her Mrs. Miracle)
is working in the toy department at Finley's, the last
family-owned department store in Manhattan.

Her boss (who happens to be the owner's son) has placed
an order for a large number of high-priced robots, which
he hopes will give the business a much-needed boost. In
fact, Jake Finley's counting on it.

Holly Larson is counting on that robot, too. She's been
looking after her eight-year-old nephew, Gabe, ever since
her widowed brother was deployed overseas. Holly plans
to buy Gabe a robot—which she can't afford—because
she's determined to make Christmas special.

But this Christmas will be different—thanks to Mrs.
Miracle. Next to bringing children joy, her favorite activity
is giving romance a nudge. Fortunately, Jake and Holly
are receptive to her "hints." And thanks to Mrs. Miracle,
Christmas takes on new meaning for Jake. For all of them!

Call Me Mrs. Miracle

Available wherever books are sold
September 28!

www.MIRABooks.com

MDM2819